"S—am? Is—is that really you?"

Sam couldn't move. *Not Jackie. Not here in Juneau.*

"Wh–what are you doing in Alaska?"

He gaped at her. "I'm—I'm moving here," he finally said, as visions of the woman he once knew so well flooded his mind.

She bowed her head as her palm went to her chest, and she let out a long, slow sigh. "This can't be happening."

Sam fumbled for words. "Surely you don't live here."

Jackie nodded, her gaze still directed toward the ground. "Yes. Juneau has been my home since—"

JOYCE LIVINGSTON has done many things in her life (in addition to being a wife, mother of six, and grandmother to oodles of grandkids, all of whom she loves dearly), from being a television broadcaster for eighteen years, to lecturing and teaching on quilting and sewing, to writing magazine articles on a variety of subjects. She's danced with Lawrence Welk, ice-skated with a chimpanzee, had bottles broken over her head by stuntmen, interviewed hundreds of celebrities and controversial figures, and done many other interesting and unusual things. But now, when she isn't off traveling to wonderful and exotic places as a part-time tour escort, her days are spent sitting in front of her computer, creating stories. She feels her writing is a ministry and a calling from God, and she hopes Heartsong Presents readers will be touched and uplifted by what she writes. Joyce loves to hear from her readers and invites you to visit her on the Internet at www.joycelivingston.com.

Books by Joyce Livingston

HEARTSONG PRESENTS
HP353—Ice Castle
HP382—The Bride Wore Boots
HP437—Northern Exposure
HP482—Hand Quilted with Love
HP516—Lucy's Quilt
HP521—Be My Valentine
HP546—Love Is Kind

The Baby Quilt

Joyce Livingston

Heartsong Presents

To our readers who have had miscarriages and to some very special women in my life who have also lost their babies in this dreadful way: Dawn Lee, Dari Lynn, Cat, Tammie, Willow, and Melissa. Losing a child has to be one of life's most traumatic tragedies. My heart goes out to all of you. May God give you a peace that only He can give.

A special thanks goes to Morgan Chilson, who was a tremendous help with the final revisions on *The Baby Quilt*. Thanks, Morgan—you're terrific!

A note from the author:
I love to hear from my readers! You may correspond with me by writing:

Joyce Livingston
Author Relations
PO Box 719
Uhrichsville, OH 44683

ISBN 1-59310-046-9

THE BABY QUILT

Our mission is to publish an distribute inspirational products offering exceptional value and biblical encouragement to the masses.

All Scripture quotations are taken from the King James Version of the Bible.

PRINTED IN THE U.S.A.

one

Jackie Reid's eyes misted over as she stared at the vast array of hand-quilting thread lining the shelves of the Bear Paw Quilt Shop. So many colors from which to choose, so many varieties. Trying to keep her emotions in check, she picked up a spool and rotated it in her fingers. She'd spent weeks planning her project, and now she was ready to begin. The color had to be just right. *Blue might be nice since—*

"Is that for the new block of the month you're designing for the class?"

She spun around quickly, one hand going to her chest, her heart pounding with guilt, not about to share her thoughts. "I–I didn't know you were here."

Glorianna Timberwolf wrapped an arm about her employee's shoulder and gave it a gentle squeeze. "No wonder! You seemed to be a million miles away. Whatever were you thinking about?"

"Ah—I—ah—was—wondering—if I needed to order more thread, that's all." Jackie donned a fake smile, hoping Glorianna hadn't noticed the tear that had nearly slipped down her cheek. It seemed she wore her emotions on her sleeve these days. She couldn't help it. This time of year always sent her into an emotional tailspin. Especially now that she was getting older. Her biological clock's gentle ticking seemed to clang more loudly each year.

The woman tugged on her arm. "You work too hard and

spend way too much time in this shop. Tina and I are going to lunch at the Grizzly Bear, and we want you to come with us."

Her fingers trembling, Jackie hastily put the spool back in its place and stared at the quilt shop's owner. It was hard to think of Glorianna Timberwolf as her boss. Despite their original differences, over time she had become a close friend. "I–I really shouldn't. I have to get next week's schedule posted, and our supply of batting is running low. We need to rearrange the pattern area and change the displays in the windows—"

Glorianna held her palms up with a playful scowl. "Stop! You're making me dizzy. You, Jackie Reid, need to get out more often. Just the other day, Tina and I were talking about you, and—"

"Did I hear my name?" The voice came from somewhere on the other side of a huge quilt display. Both Jackie and Glorianna turned as a lovely, dark-haired woman peeked around the corner, then sauntered toward them. "Glorianna's right. What you need is a man in your life!"

Oh, no. Not that subject again. Jackie steeled herself against the words she knew would follow Tina's pronouncement. Someone was always trying to match her up with one of the local Alaskan men here in Juneau. Why couldn't they understand? There simply wasn't room for a man in her life. Now or ever. At least, not since she'd dated Trapper Timberwolf years ago, long before he met and married Glorianna. Jackie and Trapper's relationship had been more platonic than serious.

Glorianna nodded. "I agree. I was just telling Jackie she works too hard. She needs to take a break and have lunch with us."

"Look," Jackie said, forcing another smile while trying to maneuver herself inconspicuously away from the thread counter. "I appreciate your offer, but—"

Glorianna planted her hands on her hips. "Hey, I'm the boss, remember? I do own this shop. I think I should have some say around here, even if you are the shop's manager." She pointed in the direction of the back room. "Now get your coat, and let's get out of here before some customer tries to lure you away from us."

"Yeah," Tina chimed in, moving to stand by Glorianna. "We need to have some serious girl talk."

Jackie's smile disappeared. "Please, not the we-have-just-the-right-man-for-you thing again." Even though she knew their hearts were in the right place, she wished they'd leave her alone to live her life the way she wanted to live it. *Who am I kidding? My life is nothing like I want it!*

"Aw, Sweetie." Glorianna linked her arm through Jackie's. "You deserve some happiness. You have so much to offer. You're beautiful. You have a great sense of humor. You're intelligent."

"Boring. Too demanding. Uninteresting," Jackie added with a shrug. "Besides, I am happy. I love working here at the Bear Paw."

Tina leaned close and shook her finger in Jackie's face. "Hey, who do you think you're talking to? Glorianna and I know you, Jackie. Probably better than anyone else in your life does. No one should have to depend on a job to provide happiness. And, not only that, you're selling yourself way too short. You're far from boring or any of those other things you mentioned. It's just that you've been out of circulation way too long. You need to get out of that apartment of yours and do things. Meet new people. Try new adventures. I can't believe a beautiful woman like you has never married again. Many other widows do."

"I can't believe it, either. She's right, you know," Glorianna added as she nudged Jackie toward the back room.

Jackie forced herself to grin. "What can I say? The right man has never come along. Besides, being single has its good points."

"Yeah, you're only saying that because you've been a widow so long you've forgotten. There's nothing like sharing your life with the one you love, is there, Tina?"

"That's right. I can't imagine life without Hank." Tina grinned at Jackie. "Get your coat. We're going to lunch, and you're coming with us."

Jackie cast a quick backward glance toward the thread counter. "You win. Okay. Give me a sec."

In less than a minute she was back, purse in hand, and tugging on her coat. Glorianna and Tina, still engrossed in conversation, nodded and headed for the door. Jackie waved toward one of the clerks to let her know she was leaving, then rushed to join them.

❧

Sam Mulvaney's feet were tired, and he'd had about as much of the crowd as he could take for one day. He'd never expected the Dallas helicopter show to be this big. If he didn't find an empty chair soon, he might have to resort to sitting on the floor of the big exhibition hall. Finally spotting one way off in the corner, he hurriedly made his way toward it, hoping someone else wouldn't get there first.

"This chair taken?" he asked the man seated next to it.

"Nope. The guy who was here said he was leaving. Looks like it's yours."

Sam dropped into the chair, placed his briefcase on the floor, then stuck his long legs out in front of him. "I thought I was pretty physically fit, but I'm sure not used to this much walking. My dogs are killing me."

The man turned slightly toward him with a chuckle. "Yeah, mine, too, although I hate to admit it."

"You a pilot?"

His seat companion grinned. "Yep. You?"

Sam nodded. "Sure am. Learned to fly these babies in the army. Been out a year, and I'm still trying to decide what I want to be when I grow up."

"Career military?"

"Yep. Retired after twenty years of service. You ever in the military?"

The man shook his head as the corners of his mouth lifted in a smile that could barely be seen through his thick beard. "Naw, though I considered it at one time. Things weren't goin' so well in my life, and I thought I needed to make a drastic change."

"Being in the military is a drastic change until you get used to it." Sam grinned, shifted his position in the seat, and stuck out his hand. "I'm Sam Mulvaney."

The bearded man took his hand and shook it vigorously. "Trapper. Trapper Timberwolf. Nice to meet you, Sam."

"Umm, Timberwolf. That's an unusual name. Don't think I've ever run into a Timberwolf before. Not even in the army, and believe me, I've heard some unusual names. Where you from?"

Trapper's thumb and forefinger smoothed his dark mustache. "Alaska. Juneau, to be exact. There're a few Timberwolfs up there. None I'm related to, other than my dad and mom."

Sam reared back, his brows raised. "Alaska? Now that's one place I've always wanted to go. I bet it's beautiful up there."

The man's face lit up. "Oh, yes. It's God's country. There's no place like it. You need to visit sometime."

"Yeah, I'd like to," Sam said slowly, trying to remember if he'd ever known anyone who had actually lived in Alaska. "You said you were a pilot. I guess since you're at this Helicopter Association International Show, you must fly a helicopter."

Trapper shook his head. "Nope. I fly a seaplane. A six-passenger de Havilland DHC 2 Beaver."

"Hey, I learned to fly seaplanes when I was stationed at the Fort Lewis, Washington, army base. A Cessna 185 Skywagon. I sure enjoyed flying those things. Sweet model. I've never flown one as big as the de Havilland Beaver." Sam leaned back and crossed his ankles, his feet feeling much better now that he'd taken a load off them. "I've heard seaplanes are as common as those big, old mosquitoes you have in Alaska. Is that true?"

Trapper huffed. "I have to admit our Alaskan mosquitoes deserve every bad comment you've heard about them. They're huge! But, yes. What you've heard is true. Seaplanes are about as common as mosquitoes. But up there we really need them. They're a necessity."

Sam paused, thinking over the stranger's words. "You own your own plane, or do you work for someone?"

Trapper smiled proudly. "It's mine. I formed my own company a number of years ago, but I'm looking to expand. God has been good to me, and I have more seaplane business than one man can handle."

Startled by his words, Sam stared at Trapper. Most of the

men he knew didn't go around talking about God the way his new acquaintance did. They used His name in a derogatory way. He'd done the same thing himself, though he wasn't proud of it.

"I'm thankful, of course, that people want to work with me," Trapper went on, "but it does present a problem. I can't be in two places at once. I'm losing business I wish I could keep."

Sam frowned. "I'd think with that many seaplanes in the area it'd be a simple matter to hire a pilot to work with you."

"Ah, but that would mean buying another seaplane. At this point I'm not sure a purchase like that would be wise. For two reasons. Number one: Seaplanes aren't cheap. Number two: I'm pretty picky. I would never hire just any old pilot. He'd have to be not only highly qualified as a pilot, but I'd hope he would share my values."

"I don't get it." Sam extended his hands, palms up. "Why are you here at the helicopter show if your business is flying seaplanes?"

"Because I've decided, instead of adding another seaplane, it might be smarter if I got me a helicopter. I'm sure you know, although it seems a lot of folks don't, that Juneau is only accessible by air or sea. So big trucks and cranes are hard to come by. More and more, as in the other states, heavy-duty helicopters are being used to carry equipment to sites and lower it into place. I've done quite a bit of research, and I'm convinced I could more than double my business the first year with a helicopter. So," he said, gesturing toward only a small portion of the mammoth display that covered acres of ground, "I came down here to check them out."

"Well, you came to the right place." Sam let his gaze wander across the crowded hall. "If you have any questions, this is the place to get answers. Seen anything yet that might work for you?"

"Maybe. I'm going to have me another look tomorrow." Trapper stood, stretching first one arm, then the other, before bending and picking up his briefcase. "But right now I'm goin' back to the hotel, have me a big, juicy steak in the lobby restaurant, then head for my room, where I can sit in the comfort of an easy chair and read all those brochures I picked up."

Sam stood, too. "Sounds like a great idea. I've had about all I can take for one day." He picked up his own briefcase. "Where you staying?"

Trapper laughed. "The closest place I could find. The Hyatt Regency over on Reunion Boulevard. At least they're providing HAI shuttles from here to the hotel—if you can get one, with this crowd."

"Hey, that's where I'm staying. Wanna share a cab?"

"Sure, but only if you're interested in having a steak with me."

Sam nodded as the two men made their way through the throng toward the exit doors. "Sounds good to me. I haven't made any plans for dinner."

"Air!" Trapper said as he burst through the outside doors. He sucked in a big gulp and looked toward the sky. "I'm not used to being cooped up in a building all day. Give me the wide open spaces of Alaska any day."

"Sure like to see that country of yours sometime. I love winter sports. Skiing, hiking, skating, all that kind of stuff," Sam remarked as they motioned to the bellman for a cab. "Maybe someday I'll take one of those cruises I hear about on TV."

"Those cruises are nice, and I can't knock them, because the biggest share of my wife's business comes from them, but you only see a small part of our beautiful country that way."

Sam's interest piqued, he asked, "Oh? What type of business does your wife have?"

The bellman blew his whistle, and a cab pulled up in front of the pair. As soon as the two men were settled and headed for the hotel, Trapper answered Sam's question. "She owns the Bear Paw Quilt Shop. Her building faces the pier where all the cruise ships dock. When those babies unload, that whole area becomes wall-to-wall people. Those cruisers love to shop, and they flock to the Bear Paw. When the ships are in port, you can hardly move through the aisles."

"I didn't know that many women in the world made quilts. I thought it was nearly a lost art," Sam commented, thinking how little he knew of civilians' lives.

Trapper chuckled. "Far from it. You'd be surprised how many people quilt or would like to learn how. And," he said, smiling as if the shop were his instead of his wife's, "she carries a big line of gift items. Real high-quality stuff. She also carries some items made by the bush country people. I pick them up for her when I fly there to deliver medicines and other supplies those folks need. Her customers love the handmade items, and it gives the bush people some much-needed money. They have so little of this world's goods."

Sam was puzzled. "If they don't have much money, how can they afford to pay you to fly those things in to them? Isn't that expensive?"

"Pay me?" Trapper let loose a robust laugh. "They don't pay me! I volunteer to deliver it to them, and I usually spend the rest of the day helping them in any way I can. Sometimes several days."

To Sam, that arrangement didn't make sense. This Trapper fellow seemed like a savvy businessman. Why would he take his precious time, put hours on his plane, and do it for free? "Surely they pay for the things you bring them and your expenses!"

"Nope. Not a penny. For any of it."

Now Sam was really confused. "But why would you do such a thing?" He could see a big grin break out across his new acquaintance's face, even with his heavy mustache and full beard.

Trapper put a hand on Sam's shoulder and looked him eye-to-eye. "For the Lord, Man. For the Lord!"

The cab came to a sudden stop. They'd reached the hotel. "That'll be thirty-five dollars," the cabbie said, turning in his seat to face them.

❧

"Sure glad I ran into you," Trapper told Sam as he reached for his water glass. "I was dreading eating alone."

"I know what you mean." Sam glanced around the restaurant. "Looks like we were lucky to get a table. This place is packed."

Trapper laughed. "Sounds like an oxymoron, doesn't it? Eating alone in a crowd."

The two enjoyed a pleasant exchange of conversation until their meal arrived, consisting of huge steaks, baked potatoes slathered with butter and sour cream, green salads, and a basket filled with freshly baked rolls, hot from the oven.

"Umm, do those ever smell good." Sam picked up his knife as he eyed the roll basket.

"Mind if I pray?"

Sam's gaze immediately went to this stranger with whom he'd agreed to have dinner. He slowly placed the knife back on the edge of his plate. "Ah, sure. Go ahead." After watching Trapper lower his head and close his eyes, Sam lowered his but kept his eyes open, hoping those seated around them wouldn't think they were a couple of religious freaks.

"Lord," Trapper began, "I want to thank You for this food You've provided, for Your bountiful blessings, and for Sam. You're so good to us, Father, and we praise Your name. Amen."

Sam felt the corners of his mouth turn up as his gaze met Trapper's. "Doesn't seem to make any sense to thank God for the food when you're the guy who's gonna pay for it."

Trapper returned his smile, picked up his napkin, and spread it across his lap. "Ah, but He also provides my good health, which makes it possible for me to work every day. He guided me to the seaplane I should buy when I went into business. And He sends clients my way, which enables me to pay for my dinner!"

Sam let out a snicker. "I get the point. How long you been into this God thing?" As soon as he asked, Sam wished he could take his question back, realizing some folks might be offended by his flippant attitude.

"Not long enough," Trapper answered, his smile never fading as he reached for a roll. "Once, a long time ago, I was close to the Lord, then I lost my wife and turned my back on Him. Not a very smart move for someone who calls himself a Christian."

"I'm sorry—I didn't mean to pry." Again Sam wished he could take back his words. Their meal had started out so pleasantly, and he'd ruined it with his stupid remarks. "I had no right to ask you such a personal question."

Trapper took a bite of his roll, then picked up his knife and fork, poising them over his steak before looking up. "No problem. I don't mind talking about it, if you don't mind listening."

"I never know when to keep my big mouth shut. Thinking before speaking has never been one of my virtues," Sam said with a nervous laugh, still feeling guilty for his lack of acumen.

Trapper inserted the fork into his steak and used the knife to slice off a bite, then waved it in the air. "God has a way of waking a person up. That's what He did with me. Thanks to Him, I got my life back on track, and I wouldn't trade the life I have now for anything. He knew what was best for me. Once I turned control back over to Him, everything fell into place."

Sam mulled over his words. Thinking back over his own life, he wondered how different it might have been if he'd let God take control, instead of making the foolish decisions he'd made on his own.

"More coffee, gentlemen?"

Sam nodded and pushed his cup toward the waiter. Trapper did the same.

"Umm, you can't beat the aroma of a good hot cup of coffee." Sam lifted the cup and took a big whiff.

"You got that right. My wife, Glorianna, always has a big, insulated canteen waiting for me when I leave for the day. I'd hate to think how many cups of this stuff I've drunk in my lifetime."

"Does she like Alaska as much as you do?"

Trapper took a slow sip before answering. "Yes, although it took her awhile to adjust. She's originally from Kansas, but she's a true Alaskan now. You'd never be able to get her to move away."

With a smile, Sam peered at him over the rim of his cup. "Sounds like you have the perfect setup."

Trapper nodded as he placed his cup back in the saucer. "About as perfect as a man can have, I reckon. I think I'll be happy doing just what I'm doing until my dying day." He chortled. "Or until arthritis makes it impossible for me to climb up into my plane!"

Sam sobered. "Wish I could say I loved my job. This past year, ever since I got out of the army, I've been working for a guy who runs a helicopter ferrying service. Although I love the flying part, most of my days are spent transporting businessmen from one place to another. Some to attend meetings, others to look over their vast cattle ranches from the air, some to horse shows, and some just because they're bored. To them I'm only the man who sits in the pilot's seat making sure they have a safe, pleasant flight to whatever destination they've decided they want to go. Most of the time they don't even bother to say hello or good-bye. Maybe, once in awhile, one of them will give me a tip, like you'd give a bellhop for delivering your luggage to your room, but that's about it. Kinda makes a guy feel as if he isn't worth much. Know what I mean?"

"Yeah, I think I do." Trapper took another roll from the basket and tore it apart, placing one half on his plate before picking up his butter knife. "They should show some respect for you, considering all the training and hours of flying it took for you to get where you are."

Sam nodded. "Tell that to those pompous corporate execs. They think I'm nothing but a servant."

"There's nothing wrong with being a servant. But even a servant deserves respect," Trapper said with a wink before he popped another piece of the roll into his mouth.

"Well, this job sure didn't gain me any respect! I miss the excitement of my old army days and the missions I flew. I guess I should've stayed in."

"It's too bad they treat you that way, but in God's sight every man has the same value. He plays no favorites."

Sam felt himself fidgeting in his seat. Should he tell Trapper the whole story or keep it to himself? After all, he'd probably never see the man again. What difference did it make?

"Sam? You okay? You seem preoccupied about something."

"I—ah, I don't know why you'd care, or be interested in knowing, but I did something this week. Something I hadn't planned on doing. At least not yet."

Trapper tilted his head and raised a brow. "Oh? From the look on your face, I take it whatever it was, was none too pleasant."

"You're right. It wasn't, but it was for the best. I caught my boss and his secretary in a rather—what shall I say?—precarious situation? The guy has a beautiful, loving wife and four precious children! It made me so mad to think he could do such a thing that I roared into his office and quit." Sam snapped his fingers loudly. "Just like that. I told him I could never work for someone like him and look him in the face every day."

Trapper's brows rose. "Good for you. Men like that need to know they can't get away with cheating on their spouses."

Sam let out a long, slow sigh. "But that means I don't have a job."

"Sometimes a man's gotta do what a man's gotta do. I think you did the right thing. I know I couldn't work with a man knowing he'd take his marriage vows that lightly. I admire you for what you did. Not many men would've taken a stand like that."

"Well, I don't regret it, but it kinda threw my life into chaos. I've had a couple of other offers, but I'm not ready to make up my mind yet. I've even tossed around the idea of forming my own company. I have a little money saved up and some my folks left me. That's why I'm here now."

"Well, timing is everything. Maybe this is your time."

"Yeah, maybe." Sam took his last sip of coffee, placed his napkin on the table, and leaned back in the chair. "I'm stuffed. That was one good steak."

"I agree." Trapper wiped at his mouth with his napkin, then placed it beside his plate. "It's been a good, but tiring, day. I'm gonna look over my notes and the brochures I picked up at the show, then hit the sack."

Sam pulled a few bills from his wallet and placed them on the table. "You going back tomorrow?"

Trapper nodded, then reached into his own wallet. "Yeah, I want to take another look at a couple of models and maybe talk to a few representatives. I have some questions I need answered."

"So you've pretty well decided to add a helicopter to your business?"

"Seems the Lord is leading me in that direction. Now all I need to do is settle on which helicopter will be best for my purposes and find me a pilot."

Sam stood and pushed his chair close to the table. "Well, you've come to the right place. The helicopter show is—"

Trapper jumped quickly to his feet and grabbed onto Sam's arm, his eyes widening. "How about you?"

Sam frowned. "How about me? What do you mean?"

"You interested in moving to Alaska?"

two

"Me?"

Trapper motioned to their empty chairs. "Sit back down. We've got some talking to do."

Sam lowered himself slowly. "About what?"

"I'll have to pray about it, of course, but I've been thinking about the way the two of us met. You know, with God nothing is pure happenstance. You're bummed out with your job and have admitted you need a change in your life. I've decided to buy a helicopter for my business, and I'll need a good pilot. One with lots of experience. Especially one who is also a seaplane pilot. I think you might be my man!"

The eager look on Trapper's face sent Sam's mind reeling. "Me?"

Trapper leaned across the table. "Yes, you. You've said you'd like to see Alaska, and—"

"I said I'd like to *visit* Alaska." Sam shook his head. "I never said I'd like to move there."

"Ah, but that's only because you don't know what Alaska is like. You'd love it there, Man. The air is like no other place, and the mountains are beautiful. You already told me you like winter sports. Think about it!"

Sam leaned back and crossed his arms over his chest. "I–I don't know. It does sound interesting, and you're right. I would like to try something new."

Trapper pulled one of his business cards from his wallet

and handed it to Sam. "Like I said, I have to pray about this, but I have this feeling in my gut. I think God wants us to work together. Why don't you come along with me tomorrow when I talk to some of the reps? I'd like your opinion. I'm interested in that Bell 206 L III. It'll lift up to twenty-four-hundred pounds or carry six passengers. That baby is supposed to be a real workhorse. I've been looking at a used one up in Juneau that may be just what I need. Maybe you can give me some insight."

Sam stared at the man. That very morning when he'd stood in front of the mirror shaving, he'd told himself he needed a change. Something challenging. Moving to Alaska would certainly be new and challenging, no doubt about it. "Ah—sure. I'll go with you. I'd intended to go tomorrow anyway."

Once again Trapper stood, this time extending his hand. "We have a busy day ahead of us, Sam. We'd better get some sleep. Meet me here in the restaurant about seven. We'll have breakfast before we go."

Sam nodded. "Sure, seven it is."

❧

Jackie sat staring at the small stack of fabrics she'd brought to her apartment above the quilt shop, arranging and rearranging the colors but never able to come to a decision. Finally, she pushed the fabric aside with a sigh of frustration. Surely there was more to life than this! Oh, she loved her job and loved working for Glorianna, but wasn't it about time she began to think about her future? Was she planning to work in a quilt shop for the rest of her productive years? Then what? What would she do when she reached retirement age? Move into one of those assisted-living places and spend her days playing cards, listening to soap operas, and looking forward to Bingo? She shuddered at the idea. *With no one to care if I live or die?*

She wandered to the window, pushed aside the curtain, and gazed out onto Gastineau Channel. A seaplane was moving slowly across the water toward the docks, leaving a long V-shaped trail behind it. How nice it would be to glide across the water and take off into the clear, blue Alaskan sky, leaving her troubles and cares behind her. She'd gone with Glorianna and Trapper on one of their trips to the bush country, and the excitement and pleasant memories had stayed with her. The feeling of exhilaration she'd experienced at lift-off was like no other feeling she'd ever had. It was as if she were suddenly free—free from all of earth's claims on her. It was a euphoria she couldn't explain. She pressed her forehead to the glass and watched until the little plane taxied up to the dock and came to a stop. What a mess she'd made of her life. If only she could turn back the clock.

"What you need is a man in your life!" That's what Glorianna said, and so had Tina. But what do they know about my needs? A tear rolled down her cheek and dropped onto the windowsill. *They don't even know the real Jackie Reid. No one does. No one knows the ache in my heart. No one will ever understand the pain I feel. The empty spot that can never be filled. It's a part of me I'll always keep hidden.*

❧

Sam was waiting for Trapper the next morning at a table in the far corner of the restaurant. Although the two of them weren't to meet until seven, he'd been a full half hour early. He'd lain awake most of the night, thinking over the events of the past week. Exactly one week ago, at about this very same time, he'd gone into the office of K and K Helicopters to check on his upcoming assignments—something he did routinely. That's when he'd found his boss and the secretary together. He'd wanted to deck the guy, but he hadn't. And now he almost wished he had! But what had he done instead? Quit! Right there on the spot. Now here he was, seven days later, unemployed and considering a move to Alaska, of all places!

"Good morning!"

Sam stood quickly, thrusting his hand out to grip Trapper's. "Hello, Trapper."

After they were seated and the waitress had filled Trapper's coffee cup and refilled Sam's, the two men perused their menus, both deciding on the breakfast sampler.

"I hope you slept well," Trapper said as he placed his napkin in his lap, then carefully took a sip of the steaming hot coffee.

Sam picked up his cup and stared into it. "Not exactly."

"Oh?" Trapper's brows raised.

Sam offered a weak smile. "I couldn't get our conversation off my mind, about me moving to Alaska and joining your company."

"I thought about it a lot, too, Sam, and I prayed about it. Both last night and again this morning."

"Oh? Did God tell you anything?"

Trapper placed his cup back in the saucer and anchored his elbows on the table, steepling his fingers. "I think He did! I definitely feel Him leading us together, Sam. I don't know exactly how or why yet, but—"

"I thought of nothing else all night. I feel the same way. Almost as if I'm being drawn to Alaska." Sam bent and reached into his briefcase, pulling out a folder. "Look these over, Trapper. The day I quit my job, not knowing what I was going to do, I updated my resumé."

Trapper scrubbed his mouth with his napkin, reached across the table, and took the folder. "Hey, this is just what I needed. Sure glad you brought it with you."

Sam watched as Trapper read over each paper, occasionally looking up with a smile, sometimes even adding a satisfied-sounding, "Uh-huh."

Finally, with a shake of his head, Trapper closed the folder and handed it back to him. "I'd say that's a pretty impressive resumé. In fact, you may be overqualified for my purposes. I doubt I'll be able to pay you what you're worth and still buy that helicopter. I had no idea you had such extensive training, although I have to admit you're exactly the man I'd want to hire if I could afford you."

Sam grinned. "I thought you said your God was leading us together. Are you saying He made a mistake?"

"You got me on that one! No, I know He doesn't make any mistakes, but let's get real. I can't afford you. K and K was paying you some pretty big bucks. You could get a job most anywhere with your credentials."

Sam became serious. "Look, Trapper. Like I said, I was awake most of the night, turning this thing over and over in my mind. Yes, you're right. With my credentials and years of experience, I can probably get a job almost anywhere in the nation. And, I'll be honest, I never once considered Alaska. But being with you and seeing the way your face shows pride when you talk about it, I've come to the conclusion Alaska might be a place I'd like to live."

"But, Sam, I can't pay you what you're worth. Not and buy a helicopter, too."

"Bear with me, Trapper. Hear me out."

"Hope you men are hungry," the waitress said as she placed a big breakfast sampler platter in front of each one. "I'll be right back with your biscuits and gravy."

Trapper squared the platter in front of him. "Wow! I had no idea it'd be this big!"

"Me, either, but it sure looks good." Sam sent a smile Trapper's way. "I guess you'll want to thank your God for this, right?"

"Sure do. Do you mind?"

"Nope. Go right ahead."

This time Sam not only bowed his head while Trapper prayed, but he also closed his eyes.

"Here ya are. Biscuits and gravy. Anything else?" the waitress asked as she eyed each man.

"I think we're taken care of, but keep that coffeepot handy," Sam told her with a wink, motioning to his half-empty cup.

"Hey, this ham's pretty good." Trapper gestured toward the big slice of honey-cured ham on his plate.

Sam sliced off a small bite, forked it, then stared at it. The ham might be good, but he had other things on his mind. "As I was saying, I've given this a great deal of thought. About six hours' worth, when I should've been sleeping."

Trapper chortled as he buttered his biscuit.

"Do you remember when I said I'd even considered starting my own business? And I had a little money put back?"

"Sure, I remember."

Sam smiled, then went on. "Look, Trapper—I know how much that model Bell helicopter you're interested in costs. Even used, one will probably go for big bucks. Being in the army for twenty years I had very few expenses, and because of some earlier unpleasant experiences in my life I'd rather not go into, I've been pretty frugal with my money. Not only have I been able to save and invest wisely; as an only child I inherited everything my parents had when they passed away."

Trapper's eyes narrowed. "Are you saying you want to invest in my business?"

Sam sat up straight and tall and looked Trapper in the eye. "I want to be your partner."

❧

"Glorianna, it was the most amazing thing," Trapper told his wife as he sat on the edge of the bed and pulled off his shoes and socks. "I nearly didn't even go to Dallas, but I couldn't get that helicopter convention off my mind. It was as if God was pushing me there. Then meeting Sam like I did was the real clincher. I mean, thousands of people were in that huge convention center, and who comes and sits right beside me? Sam!"

Glorianna sat down beside him and began to massage his shoulders. "But a partner? Are you sure you want to do this? You barely know the man!"

"Umm, that feels good." He turned slightly toward her. "Think about it, Sweetheart. If someone had come and applied for the job as pilot, I would've looked over his resumé, visited with him for maybe an hour or so, made a few phone calls to check him out, and, if I liked the guy, probably hired him. Sam not only had his impressive resumé with him, but he has way more credentials than anyone I know, and the two of us did spend nearly two days together!" He reached up and cupped his wife's hand before giving it a reassuring squeeze. "Trust me, Glori. I know what I'm doing. Only God could have led us together the way He did."

"What if he doesn't like Alaska?"

Trapper huffed. "He loves outdoor sports, and he loves flying. Put that together with beautiful scenery, the wide open spaces—and what's not to like? I think the guy'll love it!" He lifted his shoulder a bit. "Ah—right there. That's it."

Glorianna's fingers moved to the spot he indicated.

"Doesn't his wife have a say in all this? Surely he's married."

"Married?" Trapper shrugged. "Don't know. I never asked him, and he never said."

She gave his shoulder a slight slap. "You never asked? You may have an irate wife on your hands, you know. Not many women appreciate their husbands coming home from a convention and telling them they're moving to Alaska!"

"Guess we'll find out soon enough. He'll be here tomorrow afternoon. I made arrangements for Sam to fly in from Vancouver with one of my clients in his King Air. He's meeting Sam there first thing in the morning."

His wife's jaw dropped as her eyes widened. "That soon?"

"Yep. I wanted him to take a look at that used Bell helicopter I'm thinking about buying before I sign the final papers. The guy really knows his stuff, Glori. He's exactly the kind of pilot I need. Even flies seaplanes." He pulled his change from his pocket, placed it on the bureau, and headed for the bathroom. "I thought we might have a little welcome-to-Alaska dinner for him at Mom's restaurant. Let him get a good taste of Mom's Alaskan salmon. Maybe Tina and Hank Gordon will come along."

She followed him and sat on the edge of the tub while he brushed his teeth. "You really think God sent this man to you?"

Trapper pulled the brush from his mouth and gave her a

frothy grin. "I've been praying about this for a long time, Glori. I'm convinced Sam is the answer to my prayers."

She gave his image in the mirror a wistful look. "I sure hope you're right. Taking on a partner is a major step."

Trapper rinsed his mouth and dried it on the towel, then, with a smile, bent and kissed Glorianna on the lips. "I know. I nearly lost you by hesitating and not making up my mind. Remember? Dumb me. I even let you and Hank get as far as the altar before I realized how stupid I'd been. I still can't believe I had the guts to snatch you away from him on your wedding day! I felt much better after he met and married Tina."

"I can't believe it, either. I'm surprised Hank will still speak to either of us after what we did to him."

"Only by the grace of God, Glori. Hank is one in a million. Maybe more. I don't know anyone who would've been willing to forgive us like that man. He's a real inspiration. That's why I want Sam to meet him. From our conversations in Dallas, although the man has principles, I doubt Sam's a Christian. Hank will be a good influence on him."

Glorianna frowned as she stood and wrapped her arms around her husband's waist. "As will you, my darling. You're my idea of a fine Christian man." She gave him a squeeze. "Even if you did purloin Hank's bride away before we could say 'I do.'"

He whirled around in her arms and quickly planted a kiss on her cheek before pulling back with a quizzical stare. "Purloin? Is that what I did?"

She giggled. "I remember my mother singing that old song when I was a kid. It said something about 'purloining my true love away.' Isn't that what you did? Purloined me away from Hank?"

He threw back his head with a laugh. "So now I'm a purloiner. I guess I'll have to look that up in the dictionary."

Glori's expression sobered. "I hope you've made the right decision, Trapper, about taking on this Sam fellow. Because if you haven't—"

"I know I have. You'll think so, too, once you've met him." He gently kissed her cheek again. "I've already called Mom and made seven o'clock reservations for our welcome dinner. Now do you want to call Tina, or do you want me to call Hank?"

❧

Sam took one final look at the crudely drawn map Trapper had given him, glanced at the sign, then turned into the parking lot of the Grizzly Bear Restaurant. *Nice place. Wow! Look at all these cars. I'll bet I'm in for a terrific meal.* He switched off the key, checked to make sure his wallet was in his back pocket, and climbed out of the rental car. He shut the door and, with a glance at his watch that told him he was nearly twenty minutes early, headed across the parking lot toward the entrance. *So far, everything Trapper told me about Alaska is true. I think I'm gonna like living here.*

His mind was so caught up with his thoughts that he barely noticed the woman who was also walking toward the Grizzly Bear's entrance, only a few feet ahead of him. That is, until she gave a slight glance back over her shoulder and he caught her profile.

"Jackie?" Sam's mind raced. Were his eyes playing tricks on him? "Is that you?"

Without responding, the woman stopped walking and stood motionless, her back still toward him.

He stared at her, unsure how he should approach her or if he even wanted to. Cautiously, he moved a few steps forward, almost hoping he'd made a mistake and it wasn't her. After all, how many five-foot-five, dark-haired, attractively dressed women could there be in Alaska? Probably thousands and thousands.

Positive he'd made a mistake, he caught up with her and was ready to apologize, when she turned to face him.

three

"S–am? Is—is that really you?"

Sam couldn't move. *Not Jackie. Not here in Juneau.*

"Wh–what are you doing in Alaska?"

He gaped at her. "I'm—I'm moving here," he finally said, as visions of the woman he once knew so well flooded his mind.

She bowed her head as her hand went to her chest, and she let out a long, slow sigh. "This can't be happening."

Sam fumbled for words. "Surely you don't live here."

Jackie nodded, her gaze still directed toward the ground. "Yes. Juneau has been my home since—" She stopped mid-sentence.

Sam could have finished that sentence for her. He was sure he knew what she was going to say next. "Why Juneau? You never even mentioned wanting to visit Alaska."

"Strange situations sometimes mean strange resolutions."

The two stood staring at one another for what seemed like an eternity to Sam.

Jackie fingered the gold chain about her neck. "Did you get married again?"

He shook his head. "No. How about you?"

"No."

He leaned a bit closer. "Isn't that the gold chain I gave you for your birthday?"

She nodded and turned away. "Yes. I rarely take it off."

"I'm surprised you still have it."

"You said you were moving here," Jackie finally said, still not looking him in the face. "Maybe it'd be best if you changed your mind."

Sam shoved his hands into his pockets and wiggled the toe of his boot in the dirt of the unpaved parking lot. "Too late. I've already made an agreement."

Jackie brushed a tear from her eye. "Oh, Sam. Please don't move to Juneau. This is my home now. I've had the same job for a number of years. I don't want to leave. I assume you're still a pilot. Surely you can find work elsewhere. Please make this easy on both of us and leave."

Her words tore at him and made him more uncomfortable than he'd been in a long time. "I already told you. I can't. Someone is counting on me."

She lifted misty eyes to his. "Juneau is a fairly small city, Sam. I've—I've—"

He frowned. "You've what?"

"I didn't want to have to explain my past or the reason our marriage failed, so when I applied for my job I told everyone I was a widow. That my husband had died in a hunting accident. With you here—"

"With me here you're afraid everyone will find out you've lied?"

She nodded.

"Why would you tell them something like that, Jackie? Surely you knew it would catch up with you eventually."

"No, I didn't think it would. Juneau is miles away from the life I once lived. I never expected someone from my past to show up here. Especially you! And I couldn't stand the idea of calling myself a divorcée. It was like admitting to a failure."

Sam shrugged. "I don't get it."

She took in a deep breath and exhaled it slowly. "Look, Sam. I arrived here with very little job experience, and jobs for people like me with a limited education were hard to come by. I'd done a little quilting when I was in 4H, so when I saw a help-wanted sign in the window of—"

Sam's palm hit his forehead, and he let out a gasp. "The Bear Paw Quilt Shop?"

Jackie stared at him, her mouth gaping once again. "How did you know that's what I was going to say?"

Sam let out a sigh as he laid his hand on Jackie's shoulder. "You're not going to believe this. Talk about coincidence. The man I signed the agreement with to become his partner is Trapper Timberwolf."

Sam felt Jackie reel beneath his grasp, and for a moment, he thought she was going to faint.

Jackie's hands went to cover her face as she began to weep openly. "Once again, you've ruined my life. Oh, Sam, why, of all places in this world, did you have to pick Juneau?"

In some ways, Sam wanted to pull her into his arms and comfort her. In other ways, he wanted to turn his back on her and remind her she was the one who had done the ruining, not him. Instead, he stood awkwardly, his hands dangling at his sides, doing nothing but watch her sob.

"I'll—I'll have to le–leave now. Th–there is no w–way Glorianna will k–keep me on as her ma–manager when she f–finds out my life has been no–nothing but a l–lie."

A silent rage swept over him. "I hate to remind you, Jackie, but your lies are what got you into the trouble in the first place. I would've thought you'd learned your lesson."

Without warning she struck out at him, her fist landing on

his chest. "I did not lie to you! I don't know how many times I have to tell you that!"

He grabbed her wrist and held on tight, hoping to avoid another onslaught, his anger with his ex-wife about to get the better of him. "You expect me to believe that? When you just told me how you've lied to your boss and everyone who knows you since you arrived in Juneau? Give me a break, Jackie. Your life has been one constant lie, and we both know it!"

"I did not lie to you, Sam!"

He stared into her mascara-stained eyes, watching the tears roll down her cheeks. Then, in a controlled voice, he said, "Let's not get into that. We both know there's no solution."

She nodded and lowered her eyes.

"Here." He pulled a freshly laundered handkerchief from his pocket and handed it to her. "You've got that black eye stuff messed up."

He watched as she pulled a compact from her purse and wiped at her eyes. He hated to admit it, but she was as beautiful as he remembered her. If anything, she was even more beautiful. *Jackie in Juneau. Unbelievable.*

Still sniffling, she gave him a weak smile. "Talk about irony. Glorianna failed to give me his name, but she invited me here tonight to help them welcome Trapper's new business partner. The last person I expected his new partner to be—was you."

"I'm sorry, Jackie. If I'd had any idea—"

"You couldn't have known."

"I guess not."

She blinked her eyes several times. "I'll turn in my

resignation tomorrow, before they have a chance to fire me."

The look on her face was so pitiful, it made him feel like a heel. "No, I'll try to break my agreement with Trapper. It'll be easier for me to leave than you."

She put a hand on his arm. "No, I got myself into this mess. I'll leave. I'll tell them I've had another job offer."

Sam looked down at her with a raised brow. "Another lie?"

"If that's what it takes. But you have to promise me you won't tell them what you know about me. I can't face the idea of Glorianna knowing she's had a liar working for her, managing her shop, even baby-sitting her children. She's been like a sister to me. I can't hurt her that way."

He shook his head. "No, Jackie. I won't let you quit your job. You're already established here. I'm not. Surely there's a way we can get around this."

"How?"

Thoughts raced through his mind. Sure, she'd lied to him, but she'd gone off and made a decent life for herself. Did he have the right to take that away from her? But what about his commitment to Trapper? His partnership with Trapper was the kind of thing he'd hoped for all his life. Was he willing to give it all up because of Jackie's lies?

"I have no other choice, Sam. I have to leave."

He took her hand in his and held it gently. "Look. Either way, I'm going to have to lie to Trapper. If you leave, I'll have to lie to keep Glorianna from finding out why you've lied to her, and I'll be lying by not letting them know the two of us knew one another before I got here. If I leave, I'll have to lie to Trapper about the reason I'm trying to break our agreement. I can't win either way."

"I'm—I'm sorry. It seems I'm always the cause of problems

in your life, when I really don't mean to be."

He shook his head sympathetically. "Okay. Here's my offer. We'll both stay, and for now we'll pretend we've never known one another. We'll be the strangers they expect us to be. I don't like this any more than you do, but I can't ruin your life over it."

She brushed away another tear and looked up at him. Sam felt as if he were looking into the face of a naughty, repentant child.

"But be forewarned, Jackie. Our deception may be discovered when we least expect it. A word, or a look, or a slipup, and it's all over. Those have a way of coming out. If that happens, you have to promise me you'll come clean with the Timberwolfs and accept the full responsibility for our lying. Is that a deal?"

"Oh, Sam. Do you mean it? You'd do that for me?"

He felt her hand cover his, and old feelings of protectiveness wafted over him, but he tried to shove them aside. "Not for you, Jackie. I'm doing this for the Timberwolfs and for me. I'm being selfish in all of this. I don't want to give up this partnership, and Trapper is counting on me. I hope you and I will be seeing very little of each other, and we can make this thing work."

"You don't know how much I appreciate this, Sam. I know how opposed you are to lies of any kind. You've always made that clear. I promise if our deception is ever discovered, I'll take full responsibility."

Sam leaned toward her and touched the tip of her nose. "If you're going to have dinner with the Timberwolfs, I suggest you go on into the ladies' room and freshen up. I'll wait a minute before I come in. We don't want anyone seeing us together. Remember," he added with a half-smile as he backed away, "act casual when we're introduced, and don't let your face give you away."

"Thanks, Sam."

Sam watched as she walked away. Except for the tearstains on her face, she was as beautiful as the day he'd married her.

❧

"Hey, Guy," Trapper said, rising. "I was beginning to wonder if you were gonna show up. You're late. Did you have any trouble finding the place?"

Sam reached out and shook Trapper's hand. "A little. I missed a turn." *There goes lie number one!*

"Oh? I guess I'm not as good a map drawer as I thought I was." He turned and gestured to those seated at the table. "Gang, this is the man I've been telling you about. My new partner and friend, Sam Mulvaney."

Sam grinned as he looked into four friendly faces.

"Sam, this is my wife, Glorianna."

"Nice to meet you, Sam. Trapper's told me all about you. Welcome to Alaska."

Sam reached out his hand. "You're every bit as pretty as Trapper said."

Trapper laughed. "And she's mine. Don't forget it." He turned to the couple seated to Glorianna's right. "These folks are our best friends, Tina and Hank Gordon."

"Ah, the Gordons. Trapper has mentioned you a number of times. I've looked forward to meeting you both."

Trapper waved his hand toward one of the two empty chairs at the table. "Sit down. Take a load off."

"Are you married, Sam?" Tina asked as soon as he was seated.

Sam grimaced. "Married? No. My wife and I divorced a long time ago."

"Well, she made it!" Trapper said with a broad smile, rising again as Jackie approached the table. "Jackie, come and meet my new business partner, Sam Mulvaney."

"Nice to meet you, Sam."

Jackie's hand was shaking as she extended it toward him. Although no one else at the table probably noticed, Sam did.

As Sam rose, he cradled her hand in his and looked into her eyes, and flashes of other, more pleasant, times surfaced from his memory. "Hello, Jackie." He pulled out her chair, waited until she was seated, then lowered himself into his own chair as he'd done hundreds of times over their married life.

"Jackie has managed my quilt shop for years, Sam," Glorianna explained. "If it weren't for her and her wonderful management and people skills, I wouldn't be able to be a full-time mom."

"So this here's Sam!" A tall, slender woman with a raspy voice who looked much like Trapper approached the table, flanked by an equally tall man. "I'm Emily, the mother of that fuzzy-faced man you've taken on as partner. And this here's Dyami, Trapper's father. Welcome to Juneau."

Sam rose and smiled at the pair, amazed by the resemblance. "Nice to meet you both."

"Sit down—sit down," Emily told him as she fluttered her hands toward his chair. "I've got some nice baked salmon waitin' in the kitchen. Your waiter will be here in a minute with your drinks." She and Dyami waved, then scurried off to chat with the restaurant full of customers.

Trapper laughed as he gestured toward his parents. "Guess

you can tell who's the talker in our family. Dad doesn't get a chance to say much."

"I like them," Sam said with a grin. It was hard to keep his eyes off Jackie as she sat next to him, and he wondered if the two of them had made the right decision. Would they be able to carry their deception off as they'd planned, or would it backfire in their faces?

Trapper gave his glass a clink with his knife. "Let's hold hands and thank God for our food."

Sam took hold of Glorianna's hand, then reached for Jackie's. How many years had it been since he'd held her hand? When was the last time? He bowed his head and listened as Trapper talked to God, much like one would talk to a friend, and he almost envied him.

"It's a treat to have Jackie here with us tonight," Glorianna said after Trapper's "amen." "I'm afraid she devotes most of her time to my shop." She sent a glance toward Tina that Sam didn't understand.

"I enjoy working at the Bear Paw, Glorianna. You know that."

His gaze went from one woman to the other as the waiter placed their water glasses on the table.

"I know you do, and it pleases me." Glorianna turned her attention back to Sam. "Tina and I have both been telling Jackie she needs to get out more often. Have a little fun. Just because a woman is a widow is no reason for her to quit living."

❧

Jackie nearly choked on her water. She swallowed hard as she set her glass on the table. It was all she could do to keep from looking at Sam, but she knew she didn't dare.

Trapper shook his head. "You'll have to forgive these

ladies, Sam. Glori and Tina are like a couple of old magpies when they get together. Always fluttering over one thing or another. Tryin' to fix things that ain't broke."

Glorianna slapped playfully at Trapper's hand. "Well, if Sam is going to be part of our little group, he'll have to get used to it."

"If you got any skeletons in your closet, Sam, you'd better come clean about them now. These girls won't be happy 'til they know every little thing about you." He gestured toward Jackie. "Isn't that right, Jackie?"

She nodded. "Yes, but only because they care about people."

Hank grinned as he took Tina's hand in his. "That they do. If anyone has a problem, these two are the ones to come to. Sometimes, when some of my clients have marital problems, I almost tell them my wife and Glorianna can help them better than I can. As an attorney I can solve their legal problems. But when it comes to personal problems, these two are better, by far, than any counselor I know of."

Trapper leaned to one side as the waiter placed his salad on the table. "Hear that, Sam? But I guess since you don't have a wife, you won't be needing their services."

Sam nodded with a slight grin. "No, I guess I won't."

Jackie shifted nervously in her seat. *Perhaps if Glorianna and Tina had been around to counsel Sam and me, we may have stayed together. Stayed together? What am I thinking? No one could've helped us, not with the way Sam felt about me.*

They finished their salads, then devoured fresh salmon, baked potatoes, green snow peas, and the wonderful bear claw rolls for which the Grizzly Bear was famous.

"Anyone for pie?" Trapper asked when their empty plates had been removed from the table.

Almost in unison, five people shook their heads.

"Well, it's been a good night." Trapper looked around the table. "Good food, old friends, and a new acquaintance who is making a new life for himself here in our beloved Juneau. Welcome, Sam."

Jackie began to relax. Dinner was nearly over, and neither she nor Sam had said or done anything that would indicate they'd ever known each other.

The group bid one another good-bye, promising to have dinner together again soon.

"Where you parked, Jackie?" Glorianna asked as they all exited the restaurant.

Jackie gestured to the far end of the parking lot, pointing toward her sports car.

Trapper pulled his car keys out of his pocket. "How about you, Sam?"

"I'm out that way, too."

Glorianna smiled at the pair. "Good, then you can walk Jackie to her car. We're parked around at the side, right next to Hank's car."

"I don't need anyone to walk me to my car. I'll be—"

Sam stepped forward and slipped his hand into the crook of her arm. "I'll be happy to."

"Good." Glorianna grabbed Trapper's arm and leaned into him as they turned away. "Thanks, Sam."

"Glad to have you with us, Sam." Tina and Hank gave everyone a wave and headed off toward their own car.

"Thanks. It's nice to be here."

Jackie tried to pull her arm away, but Sam held on. "They can't see us now. You can quit pretending."

Sam let out a slight chuckle. "Quit pretending I'm a

gentleman? I don't want you walking across this parking lot by yourself."

She stopped, pulling her arm away and firmly planting her hands on her hips. "I've gotten along without you all these years, Sam Mulvaney! Don't start pretending you care about me now!"

He grabbed onto her arm again and gently pushed her in the direction of her car as she struggled to free herself. "Hey, Kiddo! From this evening on, our lives are going to be nothing but one big pretense, thanks to you and your lies! You want to call this whole thing off?"

She quit fighting him and let herself relax. "You know I can't do that."

"Then start acting like this is the first time we've met, and let me walk you to your car."

They walked along silently until they reached her car. She pulled her keys from her purse, unlocked the door, and crawled in as Sam stood watching her every move.

"Thanks," she said, forcing a slight smile in his direction.

He pulled a pad from his pocket and scribbled something on it before folding it up and handing it to her; then he gave her a mock salute and headed for his rental car.

As he walked away, she unfolded the paper and read it.

four

Jackie stared at the note.

> *I'm staying at Grandma's Feather Bed Motel. Look up the number in the phone book and give me a call tomorrow. I think we need to talk.*

Her gaze followed him across the parking lot. *Sam. My Sam. The love of my life. Oh, he's a bit heavier, and he has a few crinkles at the corners of his eyes, but he's still the handsome man I married when I was eighteen and fresh out of high school.*

She folded the little paper and stuck it in the outside pocket on her purse, pulled the gearshift into reverse, and backed out of her place with one final glance his way. He waved as she pulled out of the lot and onto the street. *Oh, Sam, why did you have to come to Juneau?*

Her apartment above the quilt shop was dark when she pulled into the parking spot marked Manager. Looking around quickly, she grabbed her purse, got out of the car, and moved quickly up the outside stairway. Why hadn't she thought to turn on a lamp before she'd gone to dinner? She hated coming back to a dark apartment. Well, too late to think about that now. Besides, she had other things on her mind.

Like Sam.

Once inside, she made sure to lock the door behind her, turn on a lamp in the kitchen—the one she usually left on all night—and made her way to her bedroom. After a quick shower, she slipped into her pajamas, then took her purse, pulled out Sam's note, and reread it. *I'm staying at Grandma's Feather Bed Motel. Look up the number in the phone book and give me a call tomorrow. I think we need to talk.*

"About what, Sam? What else could we have to talk about?" she asked aloud, the words nearly lodging in her throat as she remembered happier times. Picnics in the park. Rowing on the lake. Holding hands in a movie. Sharing a banana split. Funny how the memory of those insignificant little things stood out above all the rest.

She remembered how she'd argued with her parents when she'd told them she and Sam wanted to get married. "You're way too young," her father had said. "It'll never last!" And it hadn't! Her father had been right—but not for the reasons he'd listed. It hadn't been money or boredom or any of the other things he'd said. If any of those things had been the trouble, perhaps they could've worked things out. Reached a compromise. Her father had been right about one thing. They hadn't known each other as well as they should have. They'd barely discussed the thing that would become the major obstacle in their marriage.

Her cheeks wet with tears, Jackie pulled out a large white box from beneath her bed and set it down beside her. She stared at the lid for a long time before removing it and pulling out six pristine white, hand-quilted blocks, the ones she'd started less than three weeks ago as a memorial to the beloved child she'd lost. "Only six more, Sammy." Her hands trembled as she sorted through the little stack, fingering each one lovingly. "Six more, then I'll add the sashings and borders, and it'll be finished."

She clutched the blocks to her bosom, patting them much like she would a crying baby to comfort it. "I love you, Sammy, my precious baby."

Rocking her body back and forth as she sat on the edge of the bed, she began to hum a lullaby. The windup clock on her nightstand ticked loudly, keeping time with her rhythm.

Finally, she placed the blocks back in the box one at a time, stacking them neatly and smoothing them out with her fingertips. *I'm glad I decided to make this baby quilt for you, Sammy. No one will ever know how I grieved at your death. Somehow just working on it and putting the tiny stitches into it helps lessen my pain.*

From a plastic bag, she pulled a square of white fabric with a quilting pattern traced onto it, along with a piece of batting she'd precut and another square of fabric. This square was also white but printed with tiny flowers. She sandwiched them together with the blue and white one on the bottom and pinned them securely with small safety pins before carefully slipping a silver thimble onto her finger. Taking a threaded needle from her pincushion, she began to quilt.

Unable to think about sleep, she quilted the entire block before placing it back in the box and attaching a long, handwritten note to it. As she lay in the darkness of her room, she thought of Sam.

❧

Sam tossed and turned. He was dead tired. It'd been a long flight from his home in Memphis to Vancouver; then he had flown with Trapper's client all the way to Juneau. Was that what was keeping him awake? Was he simply too tired to sleep?

Come on, Sam, old boy. You know the trip wasn't that tiring. After all, you slept nearly ten hours in that nice Vancouver hotel after your plane landed. And the trip in that King Air sure didn't take any work or put any stress on your body. Be honest. Seeing Jackie again after all these years is what did it.

He flipped onto his side and buried his face in the pillow. He'd thought he'd gotten that woman out of his system, but who was he kidding? Wasn't she the reason he'd never married again? Hardly ever dated?

He had to admit, even though he'd been shocked when he'd noticed her crossing that parking lot and believed he never wanted to lay eyes on her again, the old vibes were still there. Maybe being in the same city, especially one the size of Juneau, wouldn't work out as well as they'd thought it would. He doubled his fist and rammed it into the pillow. *I hate all this lying! I'm not sure I can live with it.*

❧

Jackie stared at the phone the next morning. She lifted the receiver and slowly held it to her ear, her finger poised idly over the numeric keys. Finally, she dialed.

"I'm glad you called. We need to talk."

Just the sound of his voice twanged at her heartstrings. "Why, Sam? Are you having second thoughts about our arrangement?"

"I'd rather discuss this face-to-face. Why don't you come to my motel about seven? It's out on Mendenhall Loop Road. Just off Glacier Highway, out near the airport. Park in the lot on the west side and come in through that entrance. My room is at the head of the stairs.

Number six. I'll order room service for dinner, and we can talk there."

She clutched the phone tightly. "Do—do you think that's wise? Under the circumstances?"

"You have a better idea?"

Her brain raced. With a population of only thirty-one thousand, Juneau didn't have many places you could go without running into someone you knew. "No, th–the motel will be fine."

The day seemed to drag by. Jackie buzzed through her everyday, routine tasks, but her mind was elsewhere. Even the staff noticed, and several of them asked if she was feeling well. She smiled and told them she was fine.

"Hey, whatcha think about my new partner?" Trapper asked Jackie when he and Glorianna came into the shop late in the afternoon. "Nice guy, huh?"

"More than nice, I'd say." Glorianna gave her a teasing smile. "Just about your age, too, and he's single."

"He seemed nice enough." Jackie hoped her words sounded casual. "I'm sure he's an excellent pilot. Didn't you say he'd learned to fly in the army?"

Trapper frowned. "Did I say that?"

Oh, no! Jackie flinched inwardly. Maybe Trapper hadn't mentioned that when they'd all had dinner. How would she know otherwise? Had she already goofed? "Maybe I just assumed it—since so many pilots have received their training that way," she added, trying to cover up for any mistake she might have made. She hated deceiving these people who had been so good to her, but what choice did she have?

"Well, I'm glad he's here." Glorianna slipped her arm into

Trapper's. "Let's hope his being here will take some of the stress off my wonderful husband, and he'll be home more often. The children and I miss him when he's gone." She gave Jackie a wink as the pair turned to leave. "Maybe you can show Sam around town. I'm sure he'd appreciate it."

Jackie sent her a please-don't-try-to-be-a-matchmaker look she knew Glorianna would understand.

After closing up the shop, she pulled her car into the motel parking lot at the appointed time. She took a quick glance in the rearview mirror, then warily made her way toward Sam's room, holding her breath with each step.

"Anyone see you?" he asked as he opened the door and motioned her inside.

"No, I don't think so." She glanced around the cozy room. "Nice. Do they really have feather beds?"

He gave her a shy grin. "Yes."

Jackie pulled off her jacket, then seated herself in one of the two wing-backed chairs. "Are you having second thoughts, Sam? Is that why you wanted to talk?"

"I barely slept a wink last night. I hate lying to these decent people."

She leaned back in the chair with a deep sigh. "I know. I hate it, too."

"Trapper and I went to look at that helicopter this morning. The one we're planning on buying for our business. It's exactly what we need, the price is right, and since the guy who owns it is in a financial bind, he's ready to deal." He sat down in the chair opposite her and leaned forward, his elbows resting on his knees. "One problem. We have to give him an answer by tomorrow, or he's going to fly it to Seattle and try to sell it there. I have to be mighty sure this thing is going to work out before I invest my life's savings in this deal."

"Are you—are you saying—?"

"I'm saying I'm still having qualms about this charade you and I are participating in."

Her heart pounded furiously. "So one or the other of us has to leave Juneau?"

His gaze went to the floor as he rubbed at his forehead. "I don't know, Jackie. I honestly don't know. I don't want to leave and let Trapper down, but I don't want you to have to leave, either. After all, you were here first."

She stared at him, wishing she had an answer that would be perfect for both of them. He'd hurt her once, hurt her terribly. So much that she'd even considered ending her life, but she had no desire to hurt him back. She had loved him too much at one time to do that. "Oh, Sam. I'm so sorry. The chance to fulfill your lifelong dream, and I'm the one to mess things up." She reached out and placed her hand on his wrist. It felt good to touch him again. Even in this tense situation, her flesh tingled. "You stay. I'll go."

His hand cupped hers, and her heart soared. "No. This is your home. If we can't work things out, I'll go."

She lifted misty eyes to his. "Don't go, Sam. I can't bear the idea of your disappearing out of my life again. I've missed you, Sam. I know you think lying comes easily for me, but it doesn't. But if lying will make it possible for both of us to stay in Juneau, then lying seems to be our only choice."

"I've missed you, too, Jackie. I tried to find you a number of times, to make sure you were all right. But no one seemed to know where you'd gone, or if they did, they weren't telling. I couldn't stay married to you, not after what you'd done, but that didn't mean I was no longer interested in how you were."

She wanted so much to explain that she hadn't done what he'd thought she had, but what good would it do? Hadn't she already told him a hundred times? Maybe more? He wouldn't believe her then; why should he believe her now? Especially when she was telling him she was willing to lie just to keep her job?

Sam pulled his hand away and extended an open palm. "I'm willing to do whatever it takes so we can both stay. Are you?"

She examined her heart. Of course she would. She'd do anything to keep Sam in her life now that they were able to be civil to one another again. Those last few weeks they'd been together had been miserable. His accusations had hurt her so deeply she hadn't been sure she'd ever recover. Their bitter divorce had been the final blow. She'd never forget the look on Sam's face as he'd walked out of the judge's chambers, his eyes filled with bitterness and hatred. A shudder coursed through her just thinking about it. "Yes, Sam. I'm willing. I'll do whatever it takes."

A knock on the door brought a quick end to their conversation. "Room service," a voice called out.

Although the meal wasn't the best they'd ever had, they both enjoyed it. They talked about old times, the mutual friends they'd had, Sam's final days in the army—everything but the baby.

"I'll walk you out," Sam said when she finally stood to leave.

"No, someone might see us. Can you imagine what

Trapper and Glorianna would think if someone told them they'd seen us coming out of a motel together?"

He held her jacket out for her. "Yeah, I guess you're right. Go on out, and I'll come downstairs in a minute or two and wander out to my car, as if I'm getting something out of the trunk. At least I have to make sure you get safely to your car."

"No one has checked on my safety for years, Sam. It's not necessary."

The corners of his mouth turned up slightly. "I'm here now, Jackie."

She gave him a guarded smile. "I know."

As she moved toward the door, he suddenly bent down and kissed her cheek. "I'm glad you were able to create a new life for yourself, and I want you to know I wish you well."

She nodded and tried to hold back her tears as she rushed into the hall and down the stairs, the feel of Sam's kiss on her cheek ripping at her heart.

Although it was after nine by the time she showered and dressed for bed, she pulled a new block from the box, threaded a new needle, and began to quilt, letting both her joy and frustration flow through her fingertips as she took each tiny stitch.

Something she'd never expected had happened. Sam was back in her life.

The sudden ringing of the phone made her jump, and she pierced her finger with the needle. Grabbing a scrap of fabric, she blotted at the blood as she picked up the phone. It was Glorianna.

"Hi, Jackie. I hope I'm not calling too late. I tried you several times earlier, but you must've been out. Trapper and I have invited Sam to attend church with us in the morning.

Tina and Hank will be there, too. Could I talk you into going with us?"

"I–I don't think so, but thanks for the invitation."

"Oh, come on. I think you'll really like this man once you get to know him. Tina and I have decided he's the perfect man for you. He's good-looking, single, and a real gentleman. It's time—"

Jackie pressed her eyelids together tightly. "I'm sure he's all those things, but—"

Glorianna laughed. "Do you realize, in all these years, you've never once accepted an invitation to attend church with me? We'd love to have you come with us, Jackie. Please say yes."

"Well, when you put it that way—," Jackie answered, feeling trapped but not wanting to admit it.

"Fine. Trapper and I will pick you up at nine-thirty. I'm so glad you're coming with us. We'll all have lunch together—"

"You never said anything about lunch," Jackie countered, remembering how awkward their dinner together had been.

"You have to eat, Jackie. It's only an innocent lunch. See you in the morning."

Before Jackie could add a further argument, Glorianna hung up.

❧

"What are you doing here?" Jackie's jaw dropped and her eyes widened when Sam appeared at her door the next morning. "I was expecting the Timberwolfs."

He shrugged. "I got a call from Trapper. He asked if I'd pick you up. What could I say?"

She sucked in a breath of air, not at all sure she was prepared for this, as she grabbed her purse and closed the door behind her.

The Timberwolfs and the Gordons were waiting for them in the church's welcome center. After warm words of greeting and a friendly wave from Emily and Dyami, they all made their way into the sanctuary, with Sam scooting in next to Jackie. He left a bit of space between them, for which she was glad. All went well until the worship leader asked everyone to move a little closer to their neighbors to make room for others who were looking for seating in the overcrowded sanctuary, and she felt Sam slide toward her.

She didn't know most of the music, and she was sure Sam didn't, either, since the two of them had rarely attended church during the time they were married; but she thoroughly enjoyed the congregational singing. She'd forgotten what a mellow baritone voice Sam had, and she kept remembering how he used to sing in the shower.

It was hard to sit that close to him, their shoulders touching. She could feel his warmth radiating through the flimsiness of her sleeve. Occasionally, she would slip a sideways glance at his strong profile, and her heart would flutter. Sam Mulvaney. She'd never expected to see him again, and here he was sitting beside her.

Once the six friends were all gathered around the table at the Grizzly Bear, Trapper asked God's blessing on their food. Jackie sneaked a peek at Sam just before the "amen" and was surprised to find him with his head bowed and his eyes closed.

"What did you think of the pastor's message? That man really knows God's Word," Trapper said when the conversation started up again.

Hank nodded as he reached for the basket of rolls. "Can you believe the way he explained those parables? I don't think I'll ever forget that illustration he used about the prodigal son." Then, turning his attention toward Sam, he asked, "What church did you attend in Memphis, Sam?"

Sam shot Jackie a nervous glance. "I—ah—really didn't have time for church."

Tina's brows raised. "Surely you didn't work seven days a week!"

"Now, Sweetie, don't go giving Sam a hard time," Hank inserted with a reassuring smile toward Sam. "Some guys do work seven days a week. I know I did when I was in college, and I still had trouble paying my bills!"

"Whew! I'm glad that's over," Jackie whispered to Sam as they made their way out of the restaurant and toward his car. "I don't know about you, but I was pretty uncomfortable."

Sam nodded. "Yeah, me, too. It was bad enough worrying if they were going to ask us something we'd have to lie about; but then they started talking about the preacher's message, and Hank asked me about going to church. I don't like this one bit, and I don't enjoy talking about that God stuff. I'm so afraid I'll say the wrong thing or mention something I shouldn't, or my face will give me away when I'm lying."

"I feel the same way; only I've been living like this for the past seventeen years. I've lied so long, I've nearly forgotten what real truth is." She wished she hadn't said that. It almost sounded like a confession.

"Oh, great! A flat tire!" Sam said with disgust as he squatted and glared at the back wheel. "I thought they were supposed to keep good tires on these rental cars."

Jackie leaned over him and stared at the offensive tire. "Do you want me to call someone to—?"

"I can change it myself," he half-snapped as he rose and inserted the key in the car's cargo compartment. "Just stay back out of my way."

She watched silently as he yanked off his jacket, despite the chilliness of the day, and struggled to pull the jack loose.

"You'd think those engineers would come up with a better way than this to attach a jack! It's obvious they've never had to change a flat tire."

"Ah—maybe you should undo that thingamajig," she said warily as she peered over his shoulder.

He stopped fumbling and looked up at her. "What thingamajig?"

She moved past him and touched a shiny, round metal strip. "That one."

He gave her a look of exasperation as he twisted the metal strip to one side and slid the jack free. "Dumb way to do it, if you ask me."

She swallowed a giggle but didn't respond.

"Now where'd they put the handle?" he asked, still holding the jack while shoving a toolbox, a bag of rags, and a shovel to one side.

Men! Jackie leaned over and pulled a metal bar from along the side of the cargo area's wall. "This it?"

Sam nodded his head, a deep frown cutting into his forehead. "Thanks."

But as he inserted the metal bar into the side of the jack, it was at once obvious the two pieces weren't meant to go together. "Can you believe it? Someone put the wrong size handle in here!"

She watched anxiously as his jaw tightened, afraid he might explode from frustration at any minute. "I could call—"

"No! I'll figure something out. Just be patient!"

Okay, Buster, you're on your own!

He adjusted his position as he stared at the jack, as if by willing it he could make the handle somehow fit.

Jackie pulled her collar up around her neck, trying to ward off the slight wind. "Ha–have you ever worked a jack like this one before?"

"Course I have," he said in a monotone without turning to face her.

"Maybe someone in the restaurant has a jack they could loan you."

This time he didn't turn his head; he just stared at the tire. "I said I'd figure something out."

He stood, glaring at the jack, then the handle, then the jack again. She could almost hear the wheels of his brain churning.

Typical male response.

Finally, he leaned into the trunk again, this time pulling a small roll of tape of some sort from the toolbox. "Aha! Maybe I can make this work." He snapped off a short length of tape and wound it around the handle, wrapping it as tightly as he could. But when he tried to slip it into the jack's opening it was too thick.

He gave her a macho man look as he pulled out his pocketknife and began to whittle tiny pieces from the tape.

"Hey, Man. Need some help?" a young man who looked to be in his midteens asked as he drove slowly by in a beat-up old car that looked like a refugee from a junkyard.

Sam donned a carefree smile and waved him on. "No, thanks. I've got everything under control."

The kid smiled back at him, turned his stereo on full blast, and drove off.

"Why didn't you ask him if he had a jack?" Jackie asked, her patience wearing thin.

" 'Cause I'm gonna make this thing work!" he snarled back, the pleasant expression he'd given the young man now history. "Wait in the car. No sense in you standing out here in the cold."

With one final push, he shoved the metal handle into the jack's opening. "Got it!" His face beamed victoriously.

He slipped the jack into its proper position under the car's frame and began to pump away with the handle, the car rising ever so slightly with each downward motion.

"See—I told you I'd do it," he told her, turning to her with a typically male smile as he gave the handle one more stroke. But he'd no more than uttered the words when the metal handle unexpectedly slipped from its hole.

Jackie screamed as she watched Sam's hand, still holding the handle, crash into the jack's heavy metal base.

He grabbed his injured hand and held it to him as he struggled to stand. Blood flowed from the fresh wound on the back of his hand.

Intuitively, she grabbed the silk scarf from her neck and wrapped it around his hand as he stood groaning and leaning against the side of the car.

"Is it broken?" she asked with concern.

"How should I know?" he spat out between groans as he bent over and cradled one hand in the other.

"We need to get you to a doctor," she said, trying to reach his hand to see what damage may have been done to it.

He tilted his head back and squinted his eyes tightly together. "We don't have transportation, or have you forgotten?"

"I'll see if there's a first aid kit in the glove compartment," she said, for lack of another solution, as she crawled into the car.

"They wouldn't put a first aid kit in a rental car!" he shot back at her.

She crawled out of the car with a smile. "Maybe not, but they might put one of these in there," she told him, holding up a fairly good-sized vinyl bag. "It was under the front seat."

His face still scrunched up with pain, he asked, "What is it?"

She moved quickly beside him and opened the bag so he could see its contents. "I'd say it's a small air compressor. Looks to me like one of those thingies that hooks up to the cigarette lighter."

Sam stared at the bag. "Guess I got all riled up for nothing."

"Happens in the best of families," she told him, still worried about his hand and trying to muffle her amusement. "Now, if you'll talk me through this, we'll get this tire pumped up and get you to the hospital. That hand looks like it could use a couple of stitches."

She located a small package of tissues in the car's console and placed a handful against the gaping cut on his hand. Ignoring his protests, she wrapped the blood-soaked scarf around the tissues to hold them in place. Then, taking the little compressor from the bag, she smiled up at him. "You gonna tell me how to work this thing?"

She followed his instructions as she hooked the compressor from the lighter socket to the tire valve, and soon the air was flowing through the line and the tire was inflating.

"Not too much," Sam cautioned. "There—I'd say that's about enough. That should hold it until I can change it."

She shook her head. "No, until you can get it to someone

else who can change it. From the looks of that hand you're not going to be changing any tires for a few days." She crawled into the driver's seat and motioned him inside. "I'm taking you to the hospital."

It was nearly two hours before Jackie pulled Sam's car into the parking place in front of her apartment.

"I'm sure glad you didn't break any bones," she told him sympathetically as she shoved the gearshift into the park position. "The way your weight went flying onto that hand, I was afraid you'd be walking out of that emergency room wearing a cast."

He stared at the bandage. "Yeah, me, too, and I'm thankful it wasn't my left hand. I'm not ambidextrous like some left-handed people are. I'm a total lefty."

She grinned. "I remember."

He reached into his jacket pocket with his free hand and pulled out a small plastic bag containing her blood-stained scarf. "The nurse put it in there. Guess I owe you a new one."

"Actually, you gave me this one. For Christmas the first year we were married." She took the bag from him and slipped it into her coat pocket. "I only wear it for special occasions. I–I was hoping maybe you'd remember it."

He shrugged and smiled awkwardly. "Afraid I don't."

"It's a man thing." She reached for the door handle, then gave him a smile. "Only women remember things like that."

"I owe you more than a scarf." His face took on a sheepish grin. "Thanks for being patient with me today. You know, about the tire. I guess I behaved pretty badly."

"Not too bad. Considering."

"Jackie."

"Yeah?"

"Remember that time you warned me about driving over that rocky road near our apartment and I did it anyway?"

She dipped her head and gave him a sideways smile. "Uh-huh, I remember."

"I do some pretty stupid things, don't I?"

"Umm, no more than most of us do, I guess. We've all done our share of stupid things." She pulled her coat about her and slipped out of the driver's seat. "Sure you don't want me to drive you back to the motel?"

He opened his door and crawled out, cradling his hand. "Naw, I can drive with one hand."

As they passed one another, Sam reached out and pulled her to him.

Startled, she stared up into his face, not sure what was going to happen next.

He cuffed her playfully under her chin. "You're a real trooper, Jackie Mulvaney."

She gave his arm a slight slap. "Jackie Reid, remember? Make sure you don't slip up and call me that in front of Trapper or Glorianna!"

He grasped onto her arm and leaned into her face, his warm breath falling upon her cool cheeks. "You'll always be Jackie Mulvaney to me."

She caught her breath as he moved closer, and when his lips touched hers, she felt herself yanked back to a time nearly twenty years ago. A time when she and Sam had been so in love they couldn't bear to be separated for more than an hour. She leaned against him, enjoying the sweetness of his kiss, reveling in their nearness.

Sam. Her Sam.

As his kiss intensified, she melted into him, and for that brief moment, she was his again, and it felt wonderful.

"Thanks for putting up with me today," he whispered against her lips. "Sorry for my bad manners."

"I was glad I was there for you."

He kissed her once more, then pulled away with a grin. "Yeah, me, too. I'd better get out of here."

She dipped her head and gave him a shy smile. "Please be careful driving."

He nodded as he crawled into his car. "I'm always careful."

When the phone rang in her apartment at nine that evening, Jackie assumed it was one of the staff calling in sick and took her time answering.

"Hi, it's me."

She recognized the voice immediately. It was Sam.

"I've thought long and hard about this, Jackie. Kissing you was a mistake. I got carried away, and I apologize. I've been thinking a lot about things since I got back to the motel. After our uncomfortable lunch with the Timberwolfs and the Gordons today, I've come to a decision, and I doubt you'll like it."

Her heart dropped with a thud.

"Tomorrow's the day Trapper and I are supposed to either accept or refuse the man's offer on that helicopter. I hate to go back on my word, but I have to get out of here before things go any further. I can't keep all this lying up, Jackie. It's against everything I've ever believed in."

Jackie felt her herself go weak, and she grabbed onto the chair beside the phone. "Wh–why? I thought we—"

"I'm not a liar, Jackie. I'd like to help you out, but I can't do it. I've wrestled this thing back and forth since that first night. My mind's made up. There's nothing else to talk about. Your secret's safe. I won't tell Trapper about you."

A click, and the phone went dead.

Jackie couldn't move. His words had pinned her hand to the chair. *Sam, oh, Sam.*

Eventually, she made her way into the bedroom and collapsed face-first across her bed. "God," she cried out, beating the lovely, double-wedding-ring quilt with her fists as tears gushed forth, "if—if You're r–real, and Y–You're a God of lo–love like the pa–pastor said this morning, ho–how could You let our ba–baby die? And how co–could you let S–Sam come back into my li–life again? You know how much I lo–love him. How mu–much I've always loved h–him. Now he's wa–walking out on me a–again. The pa–pain is more than I can be–bear!"

After she'd cried herself out, she pulled the seventh block from the box, removed the note she'd pinned to it, and added a few more lines, telling her precious Sammy his father had changed his mind and was going back to Memphis.

❧

Trapper grinned from his seat behind his desk as Sam entered. "Morning, Sam. Well, this is our big day! By the way, how's that hand doing? I heard about it from Glorianna. Guess she'd talked to Jackie."

"Doin' okay, I guess. Still pretty sore." Sam walked slowly across the little room, his face somber, as he pulled a folded paper from his jacket pocket and placed it on the desk before his new friend. "I hate to do this to you, Trapper, but our deal's off. I know it's not even official yet, since we haven't signed a legal contract spelling out the conditions, but I'm dissolving our partnership."

Frowning, Trapper stood, unfolded the paper, and read it silently. "This is some sort of joke, right?"

Sam shook his head. "No. No joke. I'm going back to Memphis. I have a reservation booked on the next flight out."

Trapper dropped back down in his chair and stared at him. "I thought you were as happy about this deal as I was. Did something happen to change your mind?"

Okay, Sam. Go ahead. Tell another lie. What's one more going to hurt? "I've decided I don't like Alaska after all. After hearing the local folks talk about those long Alaskan nights, I'm afraid I'd get claustrophobia."

Trapper's fingers worked at his beard. "But—you knew all about that before you came, and honest, those long nights aren't that bad. You get used to them."

Sam's good fist clenched at his side. "This place is too isolated for me. I'd go stir-crazy. Nope. My mind's made up. I can't stay."

"I'll be honest, Sam. I'm completely baffled. I knew, I just knew, the Lord had brought us together. You were an answer to prayer, Sam."

"Well," Sam said, backing toward the door, anxious to get out of Trapper's sight as quickly as possible, before he broke down and told him about Jackie. "Maybe you only thought He did. Sorry to disappoint you, but I'm outta here. I've got a plane to catch."

"If you change your—"

"Sorry, but I won't. Please give my regrets to your wife, and tell Tina and Hank good-bye for me." With that, Sam closed the door and hurried to the rental car.

❧

Still dressed in her pajamas, with her eyes swollen and red

from crying most of the night, Jackie sat staring out the window of her second-floor apartment. Earlier she'd phoned one of the ladies on the staff and told her she wasn't feeling well but would try to be in later in the day. Every bone in her body ached, and her head was killing her. In less than a week's time, her life had become a mess, and she didn't care if she lived or died.

She ignored the slight rap on the door, thinking it was probably her neighbor, an elderly woman who occasionally brought over fresh cinnamon rolls. But when she heard Sam's voice calling out her name, she rushed to the door and flung it open. "Did you change your mind? Are you staying?"

He stepped in and closed the door behind him.

five

"No, I'm afraid not. I can't stay in Alaska, Jackie. I think we both know that. I've already given Trapper my resignation."

"I–I was afraid of that."

He shifted uncomfortably, fingering his bandage. "I've never been much for believing in God and praying and all that stuff, as you well know. But sitting in that church yesterday morning I felt God's presence. Just looking at that beautiful stained glass window made me feel guilty. It was bad enough that I was lying to Trapper and Glorianna and the others, but to God?" He moved to the sofa and sat down, patting the seat beside him. "I know if I stay Trapper'll expect me to go to church with them. I don't think I could handle that a second time."

"Telling him must've been difficult."

"I felt like an idiot. I couldn't give the man a single valid reason for walking out on him."

Realizing she was still in her pajamas, Jackie quickly pulled her robe from the chair where she'd left it the night before and slipped it on before sitting down beside him. "I know what you're saying. I felt the same way. It was as if God was shaking His finger at me."

"Well, I just came by to tell you if you ever need me, you can reach me at this number." He pulled one of his old business cards from his pocket and handed it to her.

She stared at it. "You're going back to Memphis?"

He nodded. "Yeah. Aside from the years you and I lived together and my years in army housing, it's the only home I've known."

"Was Trapper angry when you told him?"

"No, but I almost wish he had been. I'd have felt better if he'd punched my lights out like I deserved." He shifted in his seat again. "You know what he said? He said he'd been sure God had sent me to him. Can you believe that?"

She nodded thoughtfully. "Yes. Knowing Trapper, I can believe it. He never does anything, no matter how insignificant it is, without praying about it first. He's a remarkable man."

"That he is, and I'm one big louse for deceiving him."

"You want some coffee? I could sure use some."

He glanced at his watch. "Sure. I've got a couple of hours before I have to head to the airport." He gave her a slight grin. "While you're in the kitchen, you might want to do something with your hair."

She felt herself blushing. She must look frightful! All that crying, and she hadn't even brushed her teeth yet, let alone combed her hair. "I had a rough night," she said simply.

When she came back five minutes later with two steaming cups of coffee in her hands, she had applied a touch of makeup to her face, her hair was combed, and she was wearing a dab of lipstick. If Sam was leaving, she didn't want him to remember her the way she had looked when he'd arrived at her apartment.

"Here you go," she said, smiling as she handed him his cup. "I'm glad you came by."

"Me, too." He sucked in a deep whiff of the rich, dark coffee and exhaled slowly. "You and I've had a pretty tumultuous life, haven't we?"

She nodded as she stared into her cup. "Good word for it. Tumultuous. But we had some good times, too." She watched as Sam blew into his cup, then took a slow sip. "I loved those good times."

"Yeah. Too bad they had to end."

She felt herself tense up. "You ended them, Sam. Not me. I never wanted the divorce. It was your idea. I loved you. I loved our life together."

He frowned over the rim of his cup. "I ended it? I think you have a lapse of memory. As I recall—"

She quickly set her cup on the coffee table with a *kerplunk*. "Why can't you believe me? I wanted that baby as much as you did!"

He banged his cup down beside hers. "Can't you stop lying, even for a moment? I remember very distinctly when I told you on our fourth wedding anniversary that I thought it was time we had a baby. And what did you say? You said, 'No, I don't want children!' Isn't that right?"

Her insides began to churn as her own anger flared. "I was twenty-three at the time! We hadn't even discussed when we'd start our family! And you were in the army! We had no idea when you might be sent off to some faraway place, if I'd get to go with you or if I'd be left at home—waiting and hoping you'd return safely! Having a baby was the furthest thing from my mind. I'd never even been around a baby. How did I know if I'd be a good mother? Or if I'd end up leaving my child with a baby-sitter most of the time like my mother did with me? I wouldn't wish that on any child! And, besides, I wanted to go to college and make something of myself. There wasn't room in our lives for a baby. At least not then!"

His eyes flashed as his thumb went to his chest. "You didn't need to go to college! I was supporting you! Me! The bread-winner of the family!"

"On army pay? Hey, don't forget I was a military brat myself!"

He leaned back on the sofa and, with a grunt of frustration, locked his hands behind his head. "I'll never forget the look on your face when that doctor said you were pregnant."

Annoyed, she shifted her weight from one foot to another. "Okay," she said, willing her voice to sound calm. "I admit it. I was upset. No, I was worse than upset. I was furious with you. I thought you'd tricked me because you wanted a baby, and you knew I wasn't ready."

"I didn't trick you, Jackie. I mean it. I hope you believe me."

She pointed a finger in his face, her anger rising with each breath. "You have the nerve to ask me to believe you, when you wouldn't believe me?"

"You didn't want that baby, and you know it!" he shot back. "Why don't you just admit it?"

"I did want our baby!" She drew a stuttering breath. "Ho–how many times do I have to tell you? Oh, not at first! I'll admit that, but—"

He spun around, his chin jutting out defiantly. "You wanted an abortion, and you got it! You didn't care what I wanted! I would've taken that baby and gladly raised it alone if necessary, but you—"

She jumped to her feet and leaned over him, firmly planting her hands on her hips. "I didn't get an abortion! How many times do I have to tell you? If you hadn't stormed off and taken that long assignment in Germany so readily, you would've been there with me, and you would've known!"

"You grumbled the entire three months before I left on that assignment to Germany!"

"Of course I grumbled. I felt lousy! I was sick to my stomach every day; my feet and hands were swelling! You knew I was miserable, but did you stay home? Tell the army your wife was having trouble with her pregnancy? No! You headed off to Germany with your flyboy friends! Flying those helicopters of yours was more important to you than your pregnant wife! I was alone, Sam. I needed you there with me!"

"Having a baby is a perfectly normal event. A lot of army wives go through their pregnancies with their husbands overseas. You were young and healthy. You didn't need me by your side every moment!" Sam rose and began to pace about the room. "That assignment meant more money. Something we needed very badly, or have you forgotten all the furniture and appliances we went in debt to buy?"

"I begged you to stay. You knew I was frightened. This was my first baby, and I was all alone. How do you think that made me feel? You were the one who begged me to have your baby, and you left me!" She plopped back down on the sofa, her head in her hands. Why couldn't he understand? Why didn't he believe her? The look on his face told her he was no more ready to believe her now than he had been then.

"I admit I wasn't ready to have a baby before that. But when I had my fifth month checkup and saw that tiny figure on the ultrasound screen, I wanted to shout for joy. I had no idea you could see things like that." She felt herself smiling at the remembrance. "I'd even heard our baby's heartbeat. Call it a natural maternal instinct or just plain loving it because it was a product of our love—whatever the reason, I suddenly knew I wanted that baby to live and be healthy."

He whirled around to face her. "You expect me to believe your melodramatics? Admit it, Jackie! You got rid of our baby! I made it easy for you, didn't I? Taking off for Germany like I did. If I had been there—maybe I could've talked you out of it. Or at least made you promise to have it and let me raise it."

Her eyes widened. "I wish you *had* been there. Maybe if you'd seen the agony and pain I suffered, you'd understand. That doctor tried to save our baby. He did everything he could. I hoped and prayed our little boy would make it!"

Sam covered his face with his hands. "It was a boy? I had a son?"

"Yes. A boy," she answered softly. The grief written on his face as he withdrew his hands tore at her heart.

He lifted his head slowly, his look of grief suddenly changing to a look of anger once more. "You did away with my son?"

"No!" She stomped her foot. "I didn't! The doctor said that many times, when there was a problem like I—"

"Problem? I know more about your problem than you think I do. I haven't told you this because a wife of one of the guys in my unit told it to me in confidence. It's the main reason I have a hard time believing you, Jackie."

Her eyes widened. "What? What could she have told you? I'd like to know."

"She said you asked her if she knew any doctors who'd quietly perform an abortion since you didn't want to go to the army doctor." He turned and headed for the door, his eyes menacing as one hand rested on the knob, his bandaged hand pointing at her accusingly. "Are you going to tell me that never happened and his wife was lying about it? What reason could she have?"

Jackie hung her head with shame at even remembering she'd done such a thing. "No, I'm not denying it. I did ask that woman about a doctor, but that was only a few days after you left for Germany, long before I heard our baby's heartbeat and the doctor did the ultrasound. I–I was upset about you leaving me."

"That's what you say now, but that's not the way I heard it!"

"Maybe the woman forgot when it was I asked her." She grabbed onto his arm. "I am telling you the truth, Sam!"

"The truth? You've told so many lies, Jackie, that I doubt you even remember what the truth is." He jerked his arm away. "I should've had my head examined for even thinking I could stay in the same city with you!"

He yanked the door open and stood glaring at her.

The tension in the room nearly crackled, and the hatred she saw in his eyes made her want to vomit. She grabbed onto his arm. "If only you'd talked to the doctor on duty at the hospital emergency room! He would've told you—"

"The emergency doctor at some little rinky-dink neighborhood hospital? If it happened like you said it did, which I doubt, why didn't you call the army OB-GYN? Answer me that!"

"Sam! I tried to explain that. I was frightened when I started hemorrhaging. All I could think about was getting to someone who could help me. The hospital was much closer than the doctor's office. I was scared, Sam! Surely you can understand that. I wanted my baby to live as much as you did!"

He yanked his arm from her grasp and stepped through the door. "Good story, but I don't believe a word of it."

She flinched as the door slammed hard behind him. The sound of screeching tires told her Sam was out of her life. This time for good.

❧

"Oh, Jackie, you'll never believe what happened!"

Jackie looked up from the ledger and fiddled with the tea bag in her cup, hoping Glorianna wouldn't notice how upset she was.

Glorianna leaned forward and let out a slight gasp. "What happened? Your eyes are all red!"

"I–I changed contact cleaner. The new stuff must've irritated my eyes." *Another lie. Where is this all going to end?*

"Well, you better let your optometrist take a look at you. Your eyes are really puffy."

Jackie nodded. "I will."

"Well, as I was saying," Glorianna went on, "you'll never believe what happened. That nice Sam Mulvaney—he walked right into Trapper's office yesterday and quit! Resigned! He gave him some flimsy excuse about Alaska's darkness and isolation. Trapper was shocked. He was sure God had led him to that man."

Jackie glanced down at the floor awkwardly. "I–I'm sorry to hear that. I know Trapper was counting on him."

Glorianna rolled a chair up beside her and sat down, still talking about Sam. "Tina and I were so excited when we met Sam. We were sure he was the perfect man for you. When we saw the two of you sitting together in church, well, we both just knew you were made for each other. Sam seemed to be one of the nicest men I've ever met. Trapper even mentioned he thought you two would make the perfect couple, and he's usually a great judge of character."

Jackie wanted to clamp her hands over her ears to block out Glorianna's words. If only she knew—

"He was such a kind and thoughtful man. I was positive he would sweep you off your feet the way Trapper did me, and you two would live happily ever after. Of course, Sam never did say he was a Christian, and that's very important if you want to have a happy marriage."

Glorianna gazed off into space. "I'm sure you remember how far Trapper and I were from the Lord when we met. I was pregnant with my deceased husband's baby, and when Trapper learned that, I figured he'd be gone forever. He wasn't sure he even wanted children, especially another man's child. But God intervened. *He* wanted us together. If two people love each other and are committed to Him, Jackie, they can work out almost anything. Trapper and I are living proof of that."

Jackie well remembered Trapper and Glorianna's courtship. At one time, she'd even deluded herself into thinking perhaps Trapper was interested in her. *Maybe if Sam and I had gone to church and become Christians and made more of an effort to understand each other's feelings, we could've made it. What was it the pastor said Sunday? That we must confess our sins and ask for God's forgiveness?*

Glorianna was so caught up in her one-way conversation that she didn't seem to notice Jackie wasn't making any comment. "I don't know how anyone can get along without the Lord in their life."

"But—what if you haven't committed any really big sins?"

Glorianna rested her hand on Jackie's shoulder. "Oh,

Sweetie, the Bible says all have sinned. That means everyone. You, me, Trapper, even that nice Sam Mulvaney!"

"So you're saying if I don't confess my sins and ask God to forgive me and turn my life over to Him, I won't go to heaven?"

"Oh, Jackie. I didn't say it. God did."

Jackie closed the ledger and folded her hands on top of it. "Someday I might want to do that, but not now. I'm not ready. I have too many other things on my mind."

Glorianna gave her a smile as she patted her shoulder affectionately. "God's always ready to listen, but don't wait too long. I'm here, if you ever want to talk."

I really don't want to discuss this now. "Look, Glorianna. I appreciate it that you're concerned about me, but you'll have to excuse me. Some new merchandise arrived this morning, and I need to go over the invoices."

Jackie left work earlier than usual and trudged her way up the steps to her apartment. She opened a can of vegetable soup, heated it in the microwave, and carried it into her living room. After eating less than half of it, she picked up the remote and turned on the TV, flipping from channel to channel without seeing what was on.

She gave up and turned it off. She carried her bowl back into the kitchen, dumped the uneaten soup into the garbage, and placed the bowl and spoon in the dishwasher. As she moved to the coffeemaker, she remembered the last time she'd used it. When she'd made coffee for Sam. Rubbing her eyes with her sleeve, she filled her cup and carried it into her bedroom, then placed it on the edge of her bed, staring at the blank wall.

Finally, she picked up the new quilting magazine that had come in the morning mail, leafed through it quickly, then tossed it onto the bed. *Oh, Sam, if only I hadn't been so childish and you hadn't been so determined.*

She moved robotically into the bathroom, brushed her teeth, and readied for bed. Why did life have to be so hard?

Oh, Sammy, my precious, precious Sammy. I did want you! You do know that, don't you? I don't know if babies go to heaven, but I hope you can hear me.

Heaven! Panic seized her. *If I don't ask God to forgive my sins, does that mean I won't go to heaven?* The thought terrified her. What if Glorianna was right? What if the only way someone could be sure she was going to heaven was the way Glorianna had explained it?

Wearily she dragged herself into bed, still entertaining thoughts of Sam. *I'll always love your father, Sammy, no matter what.*

Jackie struggled to get through each day, putting on her mask, laughing when she didn't feel like laughing, going through the usual routine of managing the shop, but every waking moment was filled with thoughts of Sam. Was he back in Memphis? Working at his old job? Did he ever think about her? Had her words made any impression on him? Would she ever see him again?

Some days she picked up the little card he'd given her and nearly dialed his number in Memphis, if only to hear his voice. But, remembering how eager he was to get away from her, she hadn't been able to do it.

The following week was no better. Finally, after realizing she had practically nothing in the apartment to eat and not wanting to go out to a restaurant alone, Jackie drove to the grocery store. She grabbed a cart and began pushing it down the aisle, grabbing things willy-nilly off the shelves, unconcerned about their fat or calorie content or if they were things she'd even eat. She just wanted to finish her shopping and get back to the sanctity of her apartment and away from the world. But as she was nearing the last corner, ready to head for the checkout counter, she heard someone on the other side of the rack asking a clerk to help him find the Swiss cheese.

Sam?

six

Could it be?

No, surely not.

Her heart racing, she rounded the corner and met him face-to-face. "Sam?"

He gave her a sheepish grin. "Yeah, it's me. I'm back."

"But—but why? I thought you were leaving for good."

"I was." He pulled a large, plastic-wrapped hunk of Swiss cheese from the shelf. "Long story. But to make it short, Trapper phoned and begged me to come back. He said he knew the reasons I gave him for leaving didn't hold water; but whatever it was, it was my business, and he promised not to pry into my life."

"But—what about the helicopter you two were going to buy?"

He shrugged. "Seems the guy with the helicopter reconsidered when we didn't make him an offer. Apparently, he'd made some unwise business decisions and had gotten himself in a financial bind. He's offered to let us have a lease option instead, and we're going to pay him a monthly lease fee, which can be broken at any time. If we decide we want to buy that helicopter, all of our lease money will apply to the purchase price. That means no money up front, except the monthly fee. Trapper suggested we give our partnership another try, so I've agreed to stay for a few months and fly the helicopter for him, at least until he can find another pilot. If things don't work out, he's agreed I can walk away with no questions asked and no obligation. How could I refuse such an offer after the man has been so understanding? Especially since, this way, I won't have to tell him my real reason for leaving."

"You really think it'll work?"

He shrugged again. "I'll be gone 90 percent of the time, so it looks like you and I won't be seeing much of each other." He glanced around but, not finding anyone close enough to overhear their conversation, continued. "I probably should've called you first and told you I was coming back. But after the way we parted, I—"

She held up her hand between them. "Don't. I'd rather not talk about it. Just promise me you'll keep our secret—that's all I ask."

"Think we can treat each other civilly?" He gave her that half-grin, the one that always made her smile. "The last thing I want is to cause you any trouble. Honest."

"I'm sure we can, if we set our minds to it." She lowered her gaze, avoiding his eyes. "At least we can try."

"I'm sure the best way to handle this is to act natural, like two people who've just met and are becoming good friends. Trying to avoid one another will probably give us away quicker than anything. Let's just go with the flow and let things happen."

She nodded. "I'm sure you're right. I'll try."

He grinned. "We'll both try."

"I'm glad you're back, Sam." She felt his hand rest on her arm, and the old tingle returned.

"Yeah, so am I."

"Your hand doing okay?"

He held it out for her to see. "It's fine now."

"See you around," she said, biting back her jagged emotions.

"Yeah." Sam tossed a box of crackers in his basket before moving on down the aisle. "See you around."

Jackie leaned on the shopping cart's handle and watched him go.

Once again, Sam was back in her life, and she wasn't sure whether to cry or shout for joy.

Putting the groceries away seemed to take forever. With so much turmoil going on in her life, she'd neglected the mundane things and had to wash the refrigerator shelves and drawers before she could place anything in them. She hadn't started the dishwasher in nearly a week, even though she'd loaded it daily with dirty dishes, and the laundry had piled up with her barely even noticing it. She set about cleaning everything until the kitchen sparkled. Not that she cared, but it gave her something to do, something to keep her mind off Sam and his unexpected return.

"So the lies will have to continue," she said aloud as she flipped the light switch to the off position and headed for her bedroom. She filled the tub, added a small vial of bubble bath, and climbed in, resting her head on the little plastic pillow suction-cupped to the tub's back. The warm water felt good, soothing, just what she needed. *Relax, Jackie. Relax. You're too uptight.* She closed her eyes, but even doing that didn't block out Sam's face.

After a good soak, she climbed out of the tub, toweled off, and pulled on a clean nightgown. She gazed into the mirror as she brushed her hair, tilting her head first one way, then the other. *What does Sam see when he looks at me?*

Does he see me as the young bride he married? She huffed. *Not likely. He probably sees me as a liar and a cheat, and he'd be right.*

She wandered aimlessly into her bedroom and turned on the lamp as the clock chimed nine. Before Sam had shown up in Alaska, she'd been busy every second. Working long hours at the shop each day, teaching quilting classes at night, attending an aerobics class, and taking part in a number of community activities. Now there seemed to be no purpose in her life. Each day was the same as the day before. Where were those challenges, those accomplishments? What had she become?

She went to the only thing that seemed to bring her solace and satisfaction these days. Sammy's quilt.

❧

"You have to come, Jackie. It's a welcome-back dinner for Sam. You're part of the six musketeers! It wouldn't be the same without you, and guess who else will be there?"

Jackie froze. *Not another surprise. No more matchmaking attempts, please.*

"The Silverbows! Dr. Buck and his wife, Victoria. You remember them. You met them when you flew up to the bush with us. Buck had some business to take care of here in Juneau, so Victoria came along. Since Buck is a pilot, too, I'm sure the men will have a lot to talk about. That'll give us women a chance for a little girl talk."

Jackie tried to remain calm. "I–I don't know—"

"It's only dinner." Glorianna grabbed hold of her arm, her eyes shining with enthusiasm. "Please! For me and Trapper? He's so excited to have Sam back. But be careful! Trapper said none of us is to mention anything to Sam about the reasons he left. Whatever they were, it's his own personal business."

Jackie remembered Sam's words. *I think the best way to handle this is to act natural. Like two people who've just met and are becoming friends.* "Sure. I–I'd love to come. What time should I be there?"

❧

Sam smiled at the group gathered around the table at the Grizzly Bear. "It was nice of you to welcome me back like this. I haven't had many friends in my life. Oh, I had buddies in the army, but none of us was ever in the same place for very long. Seems I'm always saying hello and good-bye to someone."

Trapper lifted his water glass. "To good friends."

Everyone followed his lead and added, "Hear, hear!"

"I'd like to propose a toast." Hank rose and, with a broad smile, placed a loving hand on Tina's shoulder. "We have good news, too. We're having a baby!"

Jackie shot a quick glance toward Sam, knowing how difficult it would be for her to be around Tina and a new baby after losing her Sammy. For a brief second, she caught Sam staring back at her.

"Wow! I'd say that is good news," Trapper said with almost as much excitement in his voice as if he and Glorianna were going to be the proud, new parents. "No one could make better parents than the two of you. That baby is mighty lucky."

"This baby is a gift from God." Tina smiled at her husband as she splayed her hand across her stomach. "We were beginning to wonder if it'd ever happen, but God is faithful, and our baby is developing nicely."

"Now if she can just get over the morning sickness," Hank

chimed in, beaming at his wife. "I'm finally gonna be a daddy! Can you believe it?"

"Do you have children?" Victoria asked Sam.

Jackie was sure her heart stopped beating as all eyes turned toward her former husband.

He huffed. "No, I'm afraid I'm not that lucky. I envy all of you. I've always wanted children."

Jackie felt bile rise in her throat. She was glad no one asked her that same question. She could never have answered without crying.

"Well, it's been nice to meet you, Sam." Victoria smiled at him across the table. "I want you to know you're working with a fine man." She gave her husband's ribs a playful nudge. "Trapper is almost as fine a man as my Buck!"

"Hey, I'll take that as a compliment." Trapper gave Victoria a grin. "I'll bet those kids of yours have grown since we've seen them. I know ours sure have. That little Emily Anna of ours is about as purty as they come. You'll see when we all get home tonight. I'm glad we finally talked you into staying with us instead of going to a motel. Wish you didn't have to rush off so soon. Sure you can't stay on a few days?"

Buck placed his napkin on the table and leaned back in his chair. "Nope. Duty calls. I've got a couple of boxes of medicine I need to get up to the bush people before bad weather sets in, and Tori wants to pick up the gift items the bushwomen have been making to sell in her shop." He smiled at Sam as he nodded toward his wife. "I've always called my wife Tori."

"You're quiet tonight, Jackie," Glorianna inserted when there was a lull in the conversation.

Jackie forced a smile. "I'm just enjoying being here with you. Like Sam, I haven't had many true friends in my life, only acquaintances. That is, until I moved here to Juneau."

"See, Glorianna—that's exactly what I was telling you," Tina interjected with a pleasant grin. "Jackie and Sam probably have far more in common than they realize."

Glorianna gave Tina a be-quiet frown. "Ti—na."

Trapper shot his wife a slight wink. "I'll bet the Silverbows are ready to hit the sack, Honey. They had a long flight today. We'd better let them get to bed."

"Not that long a trip." Buck snickered. "Only about 550 miles. Anchorage isn't that far from Juneau."

Trapper pointed an accusing finger in the man's direction. "Then you have no excuse for not visiting us more often."

Buck pointed his finger back at Trapper. "I think that works both ways. You need to come and visit us."

"Well, now that Sam is here, maybe Trapper and Glorianna will be able to get away once in awhile," Hank added.

Trapper rose and spread his arms wide. "I make a motion we call it a night!"

Sam stood quickly. "Again, I want to express my appreciation to all of you for welcoming me back like you have. You've made this man very happy."

Jackie's heart swelled with pride. Sam was such a gentleman. She knew how much Victoria's question had upset him, but he'd handled it with finesse. She also knew how much it had hurt him to walk out on Trapper as he had, and she vowed that, no matter what it would take to keep Sam in Juneau, she'd do it. No words or accusations, no matter how unfounded they were, could kill her love for him.

❧

Glorianna bustled into the shop several days later, all excited. "Guess what! I've signed a contract with one of those quilting machine companies. We're going to sell them here at the Bear Paw!"

Jackie listened with rapt attention. For well over two years she'd been pushing for this, and she was as excited as Glorianna. *Maybe this new project will help me keep my mind off Sam.*

"And you're going to Seattle to take the training!" Glorianna went on without missing a beat. "You'll be there three days. I already called and made plane reservations for you for seven fifteen tomorrow morning. You'll be staying at the WestCoast Grand Hotel on Fifth Avenue. The class begins the next day. Can you get ready that fast?"

Jackie's eyes widened as the words whizzed past. "Leave in the morning? Why so soon?"

"They're not holding another class for six weeks." Glorianna leaned across the counter, her fingertips touching Jackie's hand. "Oh, Jackie, please say you can make it. I'm so anxious to start offering these machines for sale at the Bear Paw. Maybe we can even teach some classes on machine quilting."

"Well—but what about—?"

"Don't you worry about a thing. I'll help out here while you're gone. You'll only be a phone call away if we run into any problems we can't handle without you. It'll do you good to get away for a few days. Come on. Say yes."

She's right. I could use a change of scenery. My life's been pretty grueling lately, even though I haven't seen Sam since his welcome-back dinner. "Okay. I'll do it!"

❧

It was nearly six-thirty the next morning when Jackie rushed breathlessly into the airport. She gave the woman her name, checked her bag, and, with her boarding pass in hand, headed for the crowded waiting area near the gate.

"Hi. I was beginning to wonder if you were going to make it."

She knew who it was before she turned around. "Sam? What're you doing here? I thought you'd probably flown up to Fairbanks with Trapper."

He stood and pointed to two empty chairs, motioning her toward them. "Naw. I didn't go. He wanted me to check out that helicopter we're going to lease and see if it needed any repairs or modifications before we took delivery."

She was puzzled by his words. "Isn't that helicopter in Juneau? What are you doing here in the airport waiting area? Are you meeting someone?"

"Nope, going to Seattle with you." He gave her a mischievous grin.

If he'd told her he was on his way to Mars, he couldn't have stunned her more. "But why?"

"Since Trapper's up in Fairbanks on that job, he won't be home for a couple of days. Seems one of his major clients called Glorianna and wanted him to hop on a plane to Seattle and pick up some parts they needed for some big machine they operate. Since he wasn't available, she asked me to go. We should be in Seattle in about four hours. I'll be able to pick up the parts and catch the last plane back tonight."

When their flight was called, Sam reached for Jackie's carry-on bag, but she grabbed it up herself. When they boarded the plane, she was relieved to learn Sam's seat was a good four rows behind hers. She allowed him to put her bag in the overhead compartment, said thank you, and sat down, buckling her seat belt. As soon as they were airborne and the seat-belt sign had been turned off, she tilted her seat back and closed her eyes.

"Sure nice no one took this seat next to you," Sam said as he sat down beside her. "The flight attendant said it was okay if I moved up here with you."

Unnerved by the way their shoulders were touching, she scooted toward the window. "Ah—sure—"

He seemed to sense her uneasiness. "I can move back, if you'd rather."

She shook her head. "No, I–I can use the company."

"Now," he said, swiveling in the seat, "tell me all about this quilting machine thing Glorianna is so excited about."

She explained what the machine could do and why it would be a good, solid, saleable item for the shop, with Sam hanging on her every word, occasionally asking a question. It was nice to be able to talk to him without an argument.

When the plane landed in Seattle, Sam grabbed her bag from the overhead compartment and ushered her into the terminal. "Well, since I don't have a suitcase to pick up, I guess this is where we separate. I'm heading on over to that parts company. Have a good time in Seattle."

She thanked him for carrying her bag, told him goodbye, and headed toward baggage claim. Sitting by him on the flight hadn't been uncomfortable at all. They'd actually had a pleasant conversation. Maybe pulling off this deception wasn't going to be as hard as they'd feared.

She checked into the hotel, ate a quick sandwich in the

little café across the street, and, having the rest of the day to do whatever she pleased, took a cab to Pike Place Market and wandered through its many unique shops.

It was nearly seven when she finally got back to her hotel room. After putting her shopping bags in the closet, she picked up the room service menu. *Do I really want to eat in my room, or should I go downstairs to the elegant restaurant I noticed when I checked in?*

The restaurant won out.

After Jackie was seated at a table near the spectacular fountain in the center of the room, she began to scan the menu.

"Hey, got room for one more?" Sam asked as he slipped into the chair opposite her.

"Sam! I thought you were flying back to Juneau tonight!"

He motioned to the waiter to bring him a menu. "So did I! Seems some of the parts I was supposed to pick up aren't ready yet. Some mix-up thing with the settings on the machines, and they're having to make them all over again. So," he said, closing the menu and laying it on the table, "I'm stuck here for a couple of days 'til they get things corrected and crank those parts out. I had to run out and buy myself a couple of shirts and some toiletries since I didn't bring a bag with me."

"How did you know I was here?"

He let out a chuckle. "I didn't! When I phoned Glorianna to see what I should do, she told me to check into this hotel and wait. I guess this is the hotel she and Trapper always use when they're in Seattle."

Although the thought upset her, Jackie couldn't hold back her grin. "You do see what they're doing, don't you?"

Sam looked perplexed. "Doing? I guess not. What do you mean?"

She let out a girlish snicker. "They're trying to get us together!"

His brows lifted as his hand went to his chest. "You and me?"

She closed her menu and leaned forward. "You haven't heard the whole story. Before Glorianna arrived in Juneau, Trapper and I—well, let's just say we were good friends. He was the first man since you who had shown any real interest in me. I took it the wrong way. So when Glorianna appeared on the scene and those two started spending time together, I actually resented her, and I guess I was pretty obvious about it. Kinda standoffish, if you know what I mean. I had the idea that if she hadn't arrived in Juneau, maybe my relationship with Trapper might have blossomed into something. Then, when Trapper and Glorianna broke up and he went to Fairbanks on a job, she and Hank Gordon became an item, and eventually, she agreed to marry Hank and accepted his engagement ring."

He gave her a surprised look. "Trapper never told me any of this. Hank and Glorianna were actually going to get married?"

"They would have, too, if Trapper hadn't come to his senses and rushed into the church as the ceremony began and snatched Glorianna away. It was the talk of the town for months. In time, Hank forgave Trapper, and they became good friends. Then, a number of years later, Tina came to Alaska, and the rest is history."

Sam's brows were raised as he shook his head. "Wow! I had no idea. I can't imagine Trapper doing anything that bold. He must've really loved Glorianna to do such an unorthodox thing. Wow!"

"I was lonely, Sam, and Trapper was such a nice man and a real gentleman. Oh, all we ever did was go to a couple of movies, but I really enjoyed his company, probably because he reminded me a lot of you."

Sam scratched his head. "No reason you shouldn't have dated Trapper. You and I *had* been divorced for a long time. Actually, I was surprised when you told me you'd never remarried. But what's that got to do with me and you?"

She laid her menu on the table and folded her hands. "Don't you see? That's the reason Glorianna is trying to turn us into a couple. After Trapper and Glorianna were married, she and I became good friends. I think she always felt a little sorry for me. Maybe she thought if she hadn't shown up, Trapper and I might have gotten together. As soon as she and I became friends, she started encouraging me to get out and date and find a good man. Then Tina came to Juneau, and she and Hank ended up getting married. Ever since then, those two women have tried to match me up with every eligible bachelor they know."

"Are you ready to order?" the waiter asked politely as he suddenly appeared at their table. "Or would you prefer I come back a bit later?"

Jackie quickly gathered her thoughts. "I'll have the petite steak, medium well, baked potato, and green beans. And iced tea, please."

"No coffee?" Sam asked with a grin.

She giggled. "Coffee *and* iced tea. I'm thirsty."

Sam took both their menus and handed them to the man. "Make mine the same, but give me the rib eye. And coffee."

"So did they?" he asked as the waiter moved away.

She gave him a blank stare.

"Did Glorianna and Tina have any success trying to match ou up with those guys?"

She tilted her head back with a laugh. "No! But they did try."

"And now they're at it again, huh, with me?"

"They mean well, Sam. Didn't you ever wonder why I vas invited to your welcome dinner and to church and hose other places? I felt like a fifth wheel. I knew what hey were doing, but what was I to do? Refuse my boss's nvitations?"

He sipped at his water, peering at her over the rim of the lass. "I'm glad you didn't refuse. It may've been weeks efore I discovered you were in Juneau if you hadn't come o the Grizzly Bear that first night."

"Well, all I'm saying is you should be prepared. Those adies are a determined pair. I think they enjoy being match-nakers!" She smiled up at the waiter as he placed their din-ner salads before them.

Sam appeared thoughtful. "Well, we are both red-blooded, nmarried people. We must've been a good match at one ime. We got married, didn't we? Maybe we'd look less suspi-ious if we played along."

His words surprised her. "You mean it?"

He shrugged. "Sure. Why not? Sure beats trying to ignore ach other."

Their conversation came to a halt as the waiter refilled heir water glasses.

"The Timberwolfs and the Gordons really are nice eople, aren't they?" Sam finally asked when they'd exhausted he matchmaking subject. "Except sometimes I wish Trapper would quit pestering me about becoming a Christian. I'm not convinced his way is the only way to get into heaven."

"I know. Glorianna does that to me, too. I've always thought if you were a good person and didn't do anything to hurt anyone, you'd automatically go to heaven when you died. But that's not what she says, and sometimes it worries me." Jackie cut a crisp slice of cucumber in half and popped it into her mouth.

"Well, I agree with you, to a point. I do think you have to be a good person, but I also think you have to do some good deeds. You know, help people, give money to the poor, give your old clothes to Salvation Army, maybe help build homes for the poor, that sort of stuff. Things like Trapper does."

"But that's not why he does them."

Sam shook his head as he reached for the basket of rolls. "He says he does those things because he's a Christian, not because they're going to get him into heaven. I've heard Hank say the same thing. Did you know Hank gives hours and hours of free attorney time to people who can't afford to hire him? He says it's his service to God."

"And that's not all," Jackie added, placing a nicely browned roll on her bread plate. "Hank goes along with Trapper some of the time and helps the bush people. Tina and Glorianna do, too."

He forked a bright red cherry tomato and twirled it in the air. "Amazing. They all have plenty of things to keep them busy, without doing that for free."

"Dr. Silverbow does the same thing. He flies his seaplane into the bush country several times a month, takes medicines he pays for himself, and doctors anyone who needs him. All for free. He even pays for the plane's gas!"

"Be careful—these plates are hot." The waiter carefully placed their dinners before them, then poured each a cup of coffee.

"Umm, these look great." Sam grinned with enthusiasm as he picked up his knife and fork and sliced off a piece of the juicy steak. "I guess we don't have to pray since Trapper isn't here."

Jackie nodded. "Guess not."

They enjoyed their steaks in near silence. Finally, she asked, "Do you think small children go to heaven? They're really not old enough to make that kind of decision for themselves."

He blotted his mouth with his napkin and cocked his head. "Hmm. I don't know. I'd think they would." Sam gave her a frown. "Did you think about that before you—?"

Jackie gritted her teeth. "I didn't—"

"Keep your voice down," he said in a mere whisper before glancing around to see if those seated at the nearby tables were listening to their conversation.

She glared at him, her voice now trembling with anger. "If you say one more word about me—"

He reached across the table and grabbed her hand, giving it a consoling squeeze. "Maybe we'd better let this subject drop."

Few words passed between them as they finished their meal.

Sam walked her to her room, taking the key from her hand and opening the door for her. "Thanks for letting me join you for dinner."

She felt as awkward as a sophomore on her first date. "I—I've always hated eating alone."

"Look," he said, lifting her chin and tilting her face up close to his, "I'm really sorry for that smart remark I made at dinner." His lips grazed her cheek. "I–I won't lie to you. I still don't believe you. But rather than *acting* like friends, I'd like for us to be real friends, especially if we're both going to continue living in Juneau."

Her heart pounded furiously. His closeness and his warm breath on her cheek were almost more than she could bear. Was he going to kiss her? *Oh, Sam, it's been so long since you've kissed me and held me in your arms.* "I–I'd like that, too."

"Maybe it'd be best," he whispered against her cheek, "if we avoided even a mention of our baby."

seven

Chaffed by his words, she drew her head back quickly. "Avoid talking about our baby? How can you avoid talking about something that was so precious but ruined your life?"

"I'm sorry, Jackie, but it seems even the mention of that baby sets us against one another. Is that the way you want it?"

"Of course that's not the way I want it, but how can I forget him?" In some ways, Sam was right. What good would arguing do? He hadn't been there when it happened; she'd been alone, and there was nothing she could do to convince him of the truth. *What I want is for you to believe me!*

"I don't expect you to forget about him, but—"

She held up her hand between them. "For the sake of peace between us and so we won't arouse suspicion, I'll try"—she bit back feelings of anguish and despair as she drew in a deep breath and finished her sentence—"I'll try to keep my emotions under control."

"Good. That's all I ask. I know you believe otherwise, but I really want us to get along." With a hint of a smile, he pulled his pen and a piece of paper from his pocket. "Give me the address where you'll be attending your class and the time you'll be finished. I'll pick you up, and we'll make a night of it."

Surprised and pleased by his request, she scribbled the information on the paper and handed it to him.

"See you tomorrow," he said, tucking it into his pocket before bending to plant a quick kiss on her cheek. "Get a good night's sleep."

Jackie leaned against the door until she heard the elevator doors close; then, her hands trembling, she hurried to her suitcase and pulled out a sealed plastic bag containing scissors, a needle and thread, a thimble, and the tenth block.

❧

Sam got off on the twelfth floor and walked briskly toward his room. He'd been so close to pulling Jackie into his arms and kissing her, instead of giving her that quick peck on her cheek. *You idiot! That would've been one of the stupidest moves you've ever made. Things are no different now than they were seventeen years ago.*

❧

Sam was already waiting in the hall when Jackie rushed out of her class the next afternoon.

"Well, did you learn anything?" He gave her a smile that was both warm and teasing.

She patted the hefty user's manual resting on her arm. "Everything is controlled by computer now. You wouldn't believe what these machines can do."

"I hope you're not on overload. I have a great evening planned."

She brightened. "Oh? Where are we going?"

Sam gave her a boyish grin. "You'll see."

"Wow!" Jackie said thirty minutes later as she and Sam stepped off the elevator and onto the observation deck of Seattle's famous Space Needle. "What a view! How high are we?"

"The visitor's book said six hundred five feet. From here

you're supposed to see not only all of Seattle but Puget Sound, Mount Rainier, and the Cascade and Olympic Mountains."

Jackie pointed off in the distance. "Oh, look! Isn't that Smith Tower down there? I think I heard someone mention it in our class today."

Sam shrugged. "Got me!"

They wandered around the deck, pausing now and then to gaze through the telescopic viewers that were available to the public, trying to locate the points of interest listed on the signs posted at each viewer.

"Hungry?" Sam asked finally, after glancing at his watch. "I made reservations for six-thirty."

She gazed up at him, still in awe of their surroundings. "Reservations? Where?"

He took her hand and led her down the stairway to SkyCity, the elegant revolving restaurant one flight down. In no time, they were seated at one of the intimate tables for two flanking the outer glass wall. The excitement she felt brought back memories of their early days together when just having a hamburger was a special occasion.

"Oh, Sam, what a wonderful place! I've always wanted to come here."

"I've heard the food is pretty good." He picked up his menu.

"We have an excellent special tonight," the waiter said as he brought their water glasses.

Sam closed his menu. "Why don't you just bring us whatever you recommend?"

The man smiled. "Excellent choice, Sir."

"That's kind of risky, don't you think?" Jackie asked with a snicker as the man scurried away.

Sam arched a brow and grinned. "Guess we'll find out when

our food arrives. Now," he said, his smile broadening, "close your eyes and hold out your hands."

She gave him a coquettish smile. "Why?"

He waggled a finger at her. "Just do it, okay? Humor the old guy."

She did as she was told and felt something soft and silky fall onto her palms.

"Okay, you can look now."

She let out a gasp of pleasure as she stared at the lovely, floral silk scarf. "Oh, Sam! It's beautiful!"

"To replace the one I ruined." He ducked his head shyly. "Remember?" He held up his hand and pointed to the healing scar.

"You didn't have to do this. I was able to rinse the blood out of the other one. But I love it." She held it to her cheek, enjoying its luxurious feel against her skin. "It—it's gorgeous. The most beautiful scarf I've ever seen and, I'm sure, very expensive."

"It looked like you. All soft and feminine and pink. I knew it was the right one the minute the salesclerk showed it to me."

She struggled to hold back tears. Before Sam had come back in her life, she hadn't cried in years. Now it seemed everything made her cry. Some days with joy. Some days from pain. Today was one of those joyful days. "Thank you, Sam," she said, reaching over to pat his cheek. "I'll keep it always."

"For an appetizer," the uniformed man said as he returned to the table, "we'll start with a sampler of prawns, grilled chicken, and grilled pineapple, served with two dipping sauces—a spicy chili sauce for the prawns and pineapple, and a curry peanut sauce for the chicken. Piled high in the middle of this is a nice Asian slaw."

"This is splendid," Jackie said as she forked up a piece of

the grilled pineapple. "I can hardly wait to taste the rest of our meal."

After the waiter cleared away their dishes, he appeared with their next course. "Now we'll have a Caesar salad and lobster bisque," he said as proudly as if he'd prepared them himself. "Enjoy."

❧

As the restaurant rotated back to face Puget Sound, the magical hour Sam had hoped for arrived, as pink and orange hues tinged with purple crept across the western sky. He had to smile as he watched Jackie's face. He was glad he'd brought her to this place.

"I–I feel like I'm floating in space," she said dreamily as she stared at the spectacular remains of the magnificent sunset.

"And now here are our entrées," the waiter said with a flourish of his hand as he lifted the beautifully garnished plates from his tray and ceremoniously placed them before them. "Northwest Salmon Wellington with pesto and lemon cream for the lady and a broiled New York Strip loin for the gentleman."

"I'm stuffed," Sam said, leaning back in his chair once their meal had been nearly consumed.

"What is that?" Jackie placed her fork on her plate and pointed to something another waiter was serving at a nearby table. "It looks like mounds of ice cream in a fish bowl, with dry ice steaming around it."

"Beats me!"

When the waiter arrived, Sam asked him about it.

"It's called a Mount Rainier, Sir, and it's always met with screams of delight. Would you and the lady like one for dessert or perhaps a lemon tart?"

"I think not," Sam said after a quick glance toward Jackie. "Maybe another time."

"Oh, look," Jackie said, leaning toward the window once the table had been cleared. "The lights are coming on all over the city. What a spectacular view!"

Sam nodded as he presented his credit card and signed the ticket. "I'd like to take one last look from the observation deck before we go. How about you?" He loved the way her face lit up when she was excited.

"Sure."

They made their way once again to the stairs and climbed back up to the deck. With the warmth of the day's sun gone, the night air was chilly. Sam slipped his arm around Jackie's waist and pulled her close, nestling his chin in her hair as they stood gazing at the sparkling jewels of the city lights below them. "This is nice, isn't it?"

"Uh-huh," she answered dreamily as she leaned against him. "Very nice."

"Think you can put up with me tomorrow night?"

She gave him a lopsided grin. "Uh-huh. Why?"

Sam brushed his lips gently against hers as he whispered, "I'd like to take you to dinner again."

It was nearly eleven before he turned out the light and climbed into his bed. He hadn't had such a good time in years. As he pulled the covers over his head, he asked himself one question: How could he hate a woman and love her so much at the same time?

Sam met Jackie after her class again the next day with a plan to spend the entire evening together. It was a plan she accepted readily.

"I thought we'd have a leisurely dinner in the hotel tonight," he told her as they drove through the streets of Seattle toward Fifth Avenue. "That okay with you?"

She nodded. "Yeah, great. It's been a really stressful day. My head is swimming with information. It'll be nice to have an early dinner and relax, but I do need to do some studying later. Since tomorrow is our last session, they're giving us a test. I want to pass with flying colors."

❧

The Terrace Garden was crowded, but the maitre d' led them to a small table for two in a far-off corner. They opted for seafood, the waiter's recommendation, then waited with anticipation as they discussed the possibilities of his choice.

"You're wearing your scarf," Sam said proudly, leaning forward as he reached out to touch the filmy silk.

"Yes, I love it. It's beautiful." As her fingers rose to stroke its softness, their hands touched.

He caught her hand in his and pulled it to his lips, kissing it gently as his gaze locked with hers. "Not as beautiful as you. You're still a knockout."

She found herself speechless and could only smile back.

"You've grown even more beautiful with the years, Jackie," he added, kissing her hand again.

Her heart came to a dull, thudding stop as she gazed into his eyes, and she was his captive. She'd always be his captive, no matter how far apart they might be.

"I still can't believe you haven't remarried, Jackie," he said in an almost-whisper as he gazed at her intently, still holding her hand.

"I've never found anyone I'd want to marry. What about you?"

He turned loose of her hand and stared off in space. "I guess I could say the same thing. I dated a few women, but none of them more than once or twice. There just weren't any sparks. It seemed like a waste of time and money."

"I'm sorry I nearly ruined your plans, Sam."

Sam gave her a confused stare. "Plans? What plans?"

She gazed at her water glass. "You know. About moving to Alaska and becoming Trapper's partner."

"I have to admit I was sure shocked when I saw you walking across that parking lot."

She offered a slight sideways grin. "I was shocked, too. I thought I was hidden away so no one would find me."

By the time they finished their dinners, they'd discussed the city and its landmarks, the weather, the Seattle Seahawks, and a number of other fairly innocuous things, each avoiding the one topic that always sent them into an argument and caused bitter words—the baby.

"Thanks, Sam. This has been a nice, relaxing evening," Jackie told him when they reached her door. "I guess we won't be seeing one another again until we're back in Juneau."

Sam grinned. "Oh, yes, we will. I picked up the parts this afternoon. They got them ready sooner than expected. I'll be going back on your flight tomorrow."

Jackie's heart played hopscotch. Being with Sam the past two days had resurrected old feelings of love. A love that had no future, a love she tried to deny still existed.

"I've really enjoyed being with you here in Seattle, Jackie." He took her key from her hand and inserted it into the lock, pushing the door open before handing it back to her.

She slipped the key into her purse and stood awkwardly staring at him. This was the man who, at one time, she had loved more than life itself. "I–I've had a good time, too." She froze as he took her hand, linked his fingers with hers, and leaned close.

"I've wanted to kiss you, you know," he whispered softly as he lessened the space between them, his face just inches from hers. "I've been fighting the impulse since that first night."

"I–I'm not so sure that would be a good idea." *But I wish you'd try.*

"Why? We're two single adults."

She dipped her head, avoiding his eyes. "We're two divorced, single adults."

He slid a finger beneath her chin, drawing her face up to his. "Precisely."

She stood motionless. Why was he taunting her like this? They both knew there was no future for them. He'd made that clear years ago. Wasn't it futile to pretend anything else?

A chill rushed down her spine as he edged closer and closer. She felt her lips moving toward his, and she couldn't stop them. Suddenly, his mouth claimed hers, and they fell into an embrace.

Try as she may, she couldn't pull away. Although he'd hurt her more than she'd ever been hurt in her life, she still loved him and wanted to stay in his arms forever. This was where she belonged. No man could ever take Sam's place in her heart or her life.

Sam kissed her again, and this time she melted into his arms willingly, loving the feel of his lips and the way his arms enfolded her. For just this moment, nothing else mattered.

"I didn't think I'd ever see you again," he said in a mere whisper when their kiss ended, the gentle expression in his eyes caressing her face. "I've missed you, Jackie."

His warm breath falling across her cheeks sent ripples down her spine. "I–I've missed you, too, Sam."

Finally, she asked, her voice low and husky, "Does this mean you believe me now?"

He pushed away slightly with a pained look. "I wish it was that simple. I'll admit I'm attracted to you, Jackie. I–I've never stopped loving you, but no matter how hard I've tried, I can't forgive you for what you did. Kissing you like that was—well, it was an idiotic idea. I shouldn't have done it."

"But I—"

He held up his hands and backed quickly into the hall. "I'm sorry. It was a mistake. I let my feelings for you cloud my judgment. I should have had better control."

"Sam, it's been over seventeen years now!" Jackie grabbed onto his arm and fought against tears as his words grabbed her heart and ripped it to shreds. "Perhaps it's time we tried to put the past behind us."

"I wish I could do that. I've really tried. But I couldn't do it then, and I can't do it now." As he took hold of her arm and stared into her face, she could see the sadness in his eyes. "If only you'd continued with your pregnancy and had the baby. Let me raise it. But, no, you took matters into your own hands. Against my wishes."

"I didn't, Sam. I didn't!"

With a final look of hopelessness and exasperation, Sam walked away, leaving her in the open doorway.

❧

She leaned against the door, crushed, feeling almost as bad as she had when Sam left her all those years ago. She'd been a fool even to consider there might be a chance for them to get back together. *You should have known better!*

Since she'd received no more communication from Sam, Jackie rode to the airport alone the next afternoon. She'd been almost glad he hadn't been in the lobby when she'd checked out after her final training session. She couldn't stand another confrontation. Already on board by the time he came onto the plane, she pretended to be reading her magazine as he walked by. The flight seemed to go on forever. By the time they reached Juneau, she was a bundle of nerves. Now what? How would they ever be able to go on with their deception, considering what had happened between them in Seattle?

Instead of going directly to the baggage claim area and taking a chance on running into Sam since he'd be picking up the big bag of parts, she stopped at the airport snack bar and ordered a cup of coffee, hoping it would calm her down. By the time she claimed her bag, he was nowhere in sight.

"Did you and Sam spend any time together while you were in Seattle?" Glorianna asked the next morning as she came into the shop.

Jackie turned her back toward her boss and busied herself straightening up the notions counter. "Aren't you more interested in hearing about the school you sent me to?"

"Well, of course, I want to hear about that. I just thought, since the two of you were staying in the same hotel, perhaps you—"

Jackie whirled around. "I wish you'd give up trying to match me up with Sam!"

"What's the matter, Jackie? It's not like you to snap at me like that. You know I meant no harm."

She rubbed at her forehead. "I–I'm sorry. I'm just tired—that's all. It was pretty late by the time I got back to my apartment last night. Even though I learned a lot, and I'm excited to tell you all about it, the school was pretty intense."

"Of course you're tired. How thoughtless of me. Why don't you take the rest of the day off? The shop's not that busy, and we can talk about your training session tomorrow."

Grateful for her understanding, Jackie smiled appreciatively. "Thanks, Glorianna. I have quite a few things in my notebook I want to go over with you. Doing it tomorrow will give me a chance to get everything organized first."

Taking her boss's advice, Jackie made her way up the outside stairway to her apartment. She unpacked the rest of her suitcase, did a couple of loads of laundry, cleaned the bathrooms, dusted and ran the sweeper, and mixed up a casserole for supper. It seemed cleaning and doing household chores always made her feel better and took her mind off things. When the casserole was done, she ate her supper in silence, placed the few dishes in the dishwasher, then picked up a romance novel she'd been intending to read. But when on the first few pages the hero and heroine had an argument and separated, she closed the book. "Too much like real life," she said as she placed it back on her nightstand and pulled the little plastic bag from the box beneath her bed where she'd placed it when she'd come home.

Oh, Sammy, what a mess we've all made of our lives.

She worked, painstakingly applying each stitch until she finished the tenth block. As she reached for her notepad and a pen, she felt a nagging tug at her heart.

Sam! My dear, beloved Sam. Why did you have to come to Juneau?

❧

Sam sat at the counter in the little café down the road from Grandma's Feather Bed, chomping on a raw carrot stick. How could he have been so foolish? He should never have kissed Jackie. That was a stupid thing to do, even if she did look so kissable, standing in that doorway, her big blue eyes focused on him, her lips beckoning him to taste them. He picked up another carrot stick and idly dipped it into the small pile of salt he'd sprinkled onto his plate. *You idiot, you're as in love with that woman now as you were the day you married her. Why don't you admit it? There'll never be another woman for you, and you know it.*

"Hey, I tried to call you at the motel. They said you might be over here."

Startled, Sam swiveled on the stool and rested an elbow on the diner's counter. "When did you get back?"

Trapper sat down beside him and took a menu from the rack. "About an hour ago. I was on my way home from the airport. But since Glorianna had left the kids with Mom and Dad so she could attend a scrapbook party some friend of hers was having, I decided to see if you wanted to grab a bite of supper with me."

"Well, I'm about finished, but I'll sit with you while you eat. Then maybe we can have a slice of pie."

Trapper placed his order, then asked, "How'd the Seattle trip go? I hear you had to wait around for those parts."

Sam nodded. "Yep, nearly three days. Big waste of time."

Trapper grinned. "Oh? I heard you and Jackie were staying at the same hotel. You mean you didn't invite that pretty little gal out to dinner?"

"Yeah, we had dinner a couple of times," Sam answered, picking up his empty coffee cup and trying to sound casual.

"She's a good woman, Sam. You could do a whole lot worse. I figured the two of you would hit it off real good."

"I don't think it'd be wise to lead some woman on right now. I have too many things going on in my life. I'm not even sure I'll be staying in Alaska."

Trapper frowned at him over the rim of his cup. "I don't like the sound of that."

"Oh, I haven't made any new decisions. We haven't even taken delivery on that helicopter. So far I like Alaska, even more than I thought I would. I just mean there's still a slight possibility things won't work out. I don't want to get attached to some woman, then go off and leave her. That's all."

Trapper nodded as he held out his cup to the waitress. "How come you never remarried? A good-looking guy like you should have his pick of women."

Because I never found another woman I could love the way I love Jackie! "I don't know. Just never did."

"You gonna spend the rest of your life alone, Sam? Somehow, when I first met you, I had you figured as a family man—married with a bunch of little kids. I was really surprised when you told me you'd been divorced. You and your wife missed the best part of life by not having children."

"Tell me about it." The words slipped out of his mouth before he could stop them.

Trapper's brows lifted. "Your wife didn't want kids?"

Sam shook his head sadly. "Nope, not even after four years of marriage."

"But you did?"

"Yeah, real bad."

"Usually it's the other way around."

The waitress brought Trapper's hamburger and fries.

He sprinkled salt on them, then doused them with ketchup. "Something on your mind you want to talk about, Sam? I get the feeling you've been holding back on me. Seems like it's been gnawing on you ever since you got here."

"I guess we all have our problems."

"Glorianna noticed it, too. At first I told her I thought you were just uncomfortable because of the way she and Tina were trying to match you up with Jackie, but—well, now, I think it's more than that."

If only you knew, Trapper. Sam stared into his cup. "I guess when I realized that matchmaking thing was going on, it did make me uncomfortable. But I thought I was keeping it to myself. Guess I didn't do a very good job."

"I think Jackie was as uncomfortable as you were. I've never seen that girl so fidgety. I've asked Glorianna to back off and leave you guys alone."

"No need. I think Jackie and I understand each other fairly well. We've talked about it some."

"Good. I'd hate to have the two of you at odds with each other." Trapper bit into his burger, then wiped his mouth with his napkin. "I hope you two can be friends."

Sam flinched. After the way he and Jackie had parted, he doubted she'd ever want to speak to him again. "I hope so, too."

"You're both important to Glorianna and me."

Sam waved a carrot stick in his direction. "Trapper, can I ask you a question?"

Trapper nodded. "Sure. Ask away."

"I've been thinking about some of the things that preacher of yours said. I remember coming home late when I was in high school and finding my daddy on his knees, praying. I always hated that sight. In my eyes it made him look like a wimp. My mama was always after me to attend church with them. Do you think they're in heaven?"

Trapper placed his napkin on the counter and began to stroke his beard. "Well, it isn't mine to say. Depends. Some people play at Christianity. I'm not saying your folks did that. Only God knows for sure. Like the pastor said, God made the rules. It's up to us to decide if we want to follow them. From the sounds of it, your folks probably did."

"So—if I want to see them again, I have to play by the rules. Is that what you're saying?"

"Exactly. So many people turn their backs on God's Son, Sam. Don't be one of them."

Sam thought long and hard about Trapper's words and about Jackie as he lay in bed that night. He loved her. There was no use denying it any longer, but he could never live with her as husband and wife, not after what she'd done. But he could stay in Alaska and keep watch over her. At least that way he'd be able to be around her, see her, and know she was safe.

If only she'd carried our baby to term—

❧

Jackie clutched the phone in both hands. "I don't mean to be rude, Glorianna, but I just don't want to go to church with you."

"Why? You said you enjoyed going with us the last time."

"If you must know, it's Sam."

Glorianna let out a little gasp. "Sam? Has he said anything out of the way or done something to offend you?"

"No, nothing like that," she was quick to say, lest Glorianna get the wrong idea. "It's—well, I know you and Tina mean well, but it's embarrassing to have your friends try to fix you up with a man." There. That sounded like as good an excuse as any.

"I'm sorry, Jackie. That's what Trapper told me. I think Sam feels the same way you do. It's just that Tina and I were so sure you two were made for each other. We meant no harm. Please say you'll come. You don't have to sit next to him. I'll make sure you sit on the opposite end of the pew from Sam. Please. I really want you to come."

Jackie squiggled her lips. "Okay, but I am not going to the Grizzly Bear with you for lunch, and I don't want you to try to pressure me."

"I promise."

The Timberwolfs, the Gordons, and Sam were already seated when Jackie arrived at church the next morning. She checked to see where he was seated, then headed down the opposite aisle, scooting in next to Glorianna, who welcomed her with a warm smile.

As usual, she enjoyed the congregational singing and the special music, but when the pastor announced his message was to be on the sin of lying, Jackie wished she hadn't come.

"Lying is a sin, no matter what the reason," the pastor was saying. "God hates lies," he added as his eyes slowly scanned the congregation. "Even those little white lies we tell so easily."

Jackie fidgeted in her seat, checking her watch often, wishing the service would end so she could get out of there. *Is Sam having the same pangs of guilt?*

"Lies are but one of the sins we commit against God," the pastor went on. "We need to confess those sins and ask His forgiveness."

As soon as the congregation was dismissed, Jackie said a quick good-bye and hurried out of the sanctuary, ignoring Sam.

Late that afternoon in the privacy of her apartment, she pulled out the study sheet that had been tucked into the church bulletin and carried it to the kitchen table. She also carried the Bible that Anna, Glorianna's mother who had owned the shop before Glorianna had come to Alaska, had given her the first week she'd gone to work at the quilt shop. She looked up the reference in the Book of Proverbs and read aloud, " 'Lying lips are abomination to the LORD: but they that deal truly are his delight." *If God hates lying lips, He must really be upset with me!* The words rang in her ears like a bell that refused to stop pealing. *I'm not only lying; I'm living a lie!*

She closed the Bible and rested her head on its cover, her tears flowing. She didn't know how long she sat there or that she'd fallen asleep; but when she woke up, the apartment was dark.

Feeling totally spent, she wandered into her bedroom and prepared for bed. But, as she lay there, wide awake, her thoughts went to Sammy and the little quilt she was making in his memory. Feeling much too restless to sleep, she turned on the lamp, pulled the eleventh block from the box, and began to quilt.

The next evening, when she heard a knock on the door, she knew, even before she opened it, that it was Sam.

eight

Sam pushed his way into the room without being invited. "I've come to a decision, Jackie. I'm going to tell Trapper about us. I'm sick and tired of all this lying. As I sat in that church yesterday and heard the pastor's words, I knew he was talking directly to me!"

"I know. I felt the same way, but please, Sam, not yet. I know the truth must come out, but I need a little time. Once you've told them, I'll have to leave Juneau and start a new life someplace else. Glorianna is as honest as anyone I've ever known, and she'll never allow me to continue to work in her shop once she finds out what a liar I've been."

He gave a dejected shrug. "That's exactly the way I expect Trapper to respond. Looks like we'll both be out of a job."

"Give me a few days, okay? I'll get my affairs in order and pack my things. As soon as they're told, I'll take the next plane out of Juneau." She put a hand on his arm and gazed up into his eyes. "Please, Sam. This is the last thing I'll ever ask of you. I just need time."

Sam took a deep breath and let it out slowly. "Okay, but one more week is the limit. Either you tell them, or I'm going to. I can't go on like this anymore."

She watched as he moved out the door without even saying good-bye. As she readied for bed, she pulled block number eleven from the box.

The next day was miserable as Jackie began to wrap up her

affairs. She worked untiringly on the shop's books, made sure there would be adequate inventory when she left, wrote farewell notes to leave behind for the staff, and wrote out checks for her end-of-the-month bills. After that, she stopped by the bank, closed out her personal account, and drew out her savings.

When Trapper's mother came into the shop, Jackie spoke to her but scurried off instead of visiting with her as she usually did, her mind on a dozen other things that needed to be taken care of before she could leave Juneau and the home she loved.

How shall I tell them? Should I call everyone together and blurt it out? Or tell Glorianna, then the others, one by one? Or let her tell them? Maybe I should just vanish and leave a note behind.

When she heard a knock on the door that evening, she hurriedly put the box she'd been packing behind the sofa.

"You can't fool me, Jackie," Emily Timberwolf said as she bustled in past her. "I can always tell when a woman's not feeling well. Especially one I know as well as I know you. You coming down with a cold?"

"I–I'm not sure. Maybe." *Another lie. How easily I tell them now.*

"I've brought you some soup, and I want you to sit down this minute and eat it while it's hot," the kindly woman told her as she grabbed hold of her arm and led her to the table.

"I–I—" The words wouldn't come.

Emily quickly pulled up a chair and sat down beside her, slipping her arm about her shoulders. "What is it, Child? You can tell Emily anything. I'd never betray your confidence."

Jackie ached to tell someone. Keeping secrets from those she cared about had taken their toll on her. Could Emily be trusted? "You—you don't know me, Emily," she said, trying to hold back her tears. "Not really."

The woman pulled Jackie's head onto her shoulder, patting her back as one would pat a crying baby. "Then tell me about yourself, Jackie. Tell Emily what's bothering you."

"I'm—I'm not who you think I am."

"Why don't you tell me all about it?"

Jackie sucked in a fresh breath of air. "I've been living a lie, Emily, and it's been tearing at my gut. I can't sleep. I can't eat. I'm miserable."

"You want to tell me about your lie?" Emily prodded softly, still patting her back.

"I–I can't. Not yet."

"I only thought it might help to get it off your chest and talk about it. The Lord knows about your lie, Jackie. Do you want me to pray with you about it?"

Tears pooled in her eyes, making it hard to see. "I–I don't think God wants to hear from me. I've never—you know—confessed my sins and asked His forgiveness, like the pastor said."

Emily shrugged. "You can do it right now, if you want."

Jackie gave her a surprised look. "Here? In my apartment? I don't have to be in the church?"

Trapper's mother gave her a gentle, understanding smile that went straight to her heart. "God doesn't care where you are when you ask for His forgiveness, Honey. He just wants to hear from you."

"I–I don't know how."

Emily took her hand, and the two of them knelt beside the sofa. "You don't need to confess your sins out loud if you don't want to, Sweetie. He already knows what they are. Just confess them in your heart. He'll hear you. You know, God loved us so much He sent His only Son to die on the cross, Jackie, for your sins and mine."

Jackie listened carefully as Emily answered each of her questions; then, still kneeling beside the sofa, she silently poured out her heart to God.

"And please, God," she added aloud after confessing her sins and asking forgiveness, "take over my life. I've made such a mess of things. I'm Yours, Lord."

"Now that wasn't so hard, was it?" Emily asked as she stroked Jackie's hair. "God created us to love and serve Him, but He wants us to do it of our own free will. Once we've turned our lives over to Him, He'll never leave us or forsake us."

Feeling a new sense of lightness and freedom, Jackie rose, then helped the older woman to her feet. "Thanks, Emily. You've always been like a mother to me. I've often wished I could be like you."

"You're a lovely young woman. Any mother would be proud to call you her daughter."

Any, except mine. "If you don't mind, I'd like to be the one to tell the others about my decision to accept the Lord."

Emily gave her hand a squeeze as her wrinkled face smiled. "I won't say a word."

They talked a bit more; then Emily kissed her cheek, took her soup pan, and departed. Jackie waved, then shut the door. She'd finally asked the Lord to come into her heart, but the lie was still there, waiting for her to confess it to those she loved. *Oh, God, give me the strength to do what's right.*

A smile crept across her face. Now she had God to turn to, and as Emily had said, He'd promised never to leave her or forsake her.

Jackie glanced at the clock and, deciding it wasn't too late, phoned Sam and asked him to come over. "I have something important to tell you."

"Can't this wait? I'm packing. Trapper and I are flying up to Skagway. I'll be back in a couple of days."

"This is important, Sam. Please. I need to see you before you leave."

While she waited, she worked on the eleventh block.

❧

All the way to her apartment, Sam pondered her words. What could be so important that she'd ask him to come over again so soon? He could think of only one reason. She'd changed her mind about telling everyone they'd been husband and wife and leaving Juneau.

"I've confessed my sins and asked God's forgiveness, and He's forgiven me!" she blurted out the minute she opened the door. "I've given my life over to Him!"

Sam did a double take. Jackie's whole demeanor was different. "When? How?"

She told him about Emily's visit and how she'd prayed with her.

"Did you tell—?"

"No! I didn't have to. She told me I could confess my sins in my heart, that God knew what they were. I didn't have to say them out loud." She grabbed onto his hand and pulled him to the sofa. "You don't know what a burden He lifted from my shoulders. It—it was as if He was right here, telling me everything would be all right, if I trusted my life to Him."

"I–I don't know why you're telling me."

"Because I want to get my life straightened out with you,

too, Sam. I've sinned against you, and I'm asking for your forgiveness."

"You—you—"

"No! I didn't abort our baby. I was only a kid, Sam, when you told me you wanted me to get pregnant. I'd never been around children. It wasn't that I was opposed to having children—ever—just not then. Not until we were both ready, but you wouldn't see my side of it. You wouldn't even listen."

He felt himself frowning. "Are you saying it was all my fault?"

She reached out and touched his arm. "No. I'm not blaming you. All I'm saying is the timing was wrong. I admit when I found out I was pregnant I considered having an abortion. Several friends of mine had gotten rid of their babies that way, and knowing how I felt, that I wasn't ready yet, they encouraged me to go through with it. It sounded like a quick way out."

"How easily you were influenced," he snapped. But instead of snapping back as she'd always done, Jackie remained calm.

"Do you remember that last day we were together? Before you left for Germany?"

He nodded.

"Your parting words to me were not—'I love you, Jackie,' or 'Take care of yourself, Jackie.' They were—'If you don't go through with this pregnancy, I'll leave you and get a divorce.'"

She blinked, and he knew she was trying not to cry.

"I was so hurt I wanted to get rid of that baby just to spite you, but I couldn't do it. Not yet, anyway. I continued going to the doctor, stayed on the diet he gave me, exercised, read the books for expectant mothers—all of it—and with each thing I became more involved. Then something happened."

Sam was sure she was going to confess to changing her mind and having the abortion, and a horrible ache consumed his whole body. He wasn't sure he could take hearing those vile words come from her mouth.

"Our baby moved! I felt it, Sam, and it was the most wonderful experience of my life. I so wanted to share that precious moment with you, but you were off in Germany, flying that helicopter. I was always jealous of that helicopter. You seemed to care more for flying than you did for me."

His own eyes misted over. He'd never realized that before.

She smiled, and it was one of the sweetest smiles he'd ever seen on her face.

"By then, I was twenty-one weeks into my pregnancy. The doctor said I should have an ultrasound procedure, to make sure things were going okay since I'd been doing a little spotting."

Her words were convincing, and for a moment, he was almost tempted to believe her story. But how easily she lied. Perhaps she'd made up this whole scenario as a cover-up. No! He wouldn't be taken in by her sweet demeanor. He wouldn't be swayed with her elaborate story about feeling the baby move and the ultrasound. Had she made all this up hoping he'd take her back? Support her now that she wasn't going to have a job?

"I don't believe you any more now than I did all those years ago. How gullible do you think I am? Did you think you could sway me with that story about that doctor telling you our baby was a boy? Come on, Jackie. I wasn't born yesterday. I did the right thing when I walked out on you."

Jackie bowed her head and mumbled to herself, and for a minute, he almost thought she was praying. Probably that story about confessing her sins was all a lie, too.

"I've heard enough. I'm getting out of here." He made his way quickly to the door. "Six days, Jackie. That's all you've got! Not a day more!"

"Sam!" she called out as she rushed to the door after him. "You need to do it, too! Confess your sins and ask God for forgiveness!"

His thumb rammed into his chest as his chin jutted out and his eyes narrowed. "Me? I'm not the one who aborted our baby. God may have forgiven you if you really asked Him to as you said you did, but I can't forgive you. I wanted that baby, and you got rid of him! Like a piece of unwanted trash."

He yanked the door shut and ran down the stairs, two at a time, eager to put as much distance between him and Jackie as possible.

❧

Jackie stood leaning against the cool metal of the door for a long time, pressing her head against its surface. Her attempt to ask for Sam's forgiveness had been futile. Not that she'd expected him to pull her into his arms, kiss her, and tell her he believed her, but she had hoped that, at least, he'd forgive her for ever considering ending her pregnancy. Her mind went back to that awful day when she'd lost Sammy. How she'd needed Sam to be with her. She'd been so alone. Only that emergency room doctor and nurse knew how she'd suffered and the agony she felt when she lost her little boy.

Eventually, she backed away from the door, locked it, and headed for her bedroom to finish the eleventh block and write her note to Sammy.

❧

Sam sat behind the steering wheel of the rental car, staring at Jackie's apartment until the lights went out in her living room. The sincerity he'd seen in her eyes ripped at his heart. Could she have been telling the truth after all? He shook his head to clear it. Of course she wasn't telling the truth! She'd been talking about having an abortion right up to the day he'd left for Germany. He'd warned her. She knew what would happen if she went through with it. She'd made up that story about having a miscarriage to cover up her guilt.

And what about the thing she'd told him about confessing her sins to God? Did she think if she confessed them her guilt would disappear and she could go on with life as if nothing had happened?

She had some nerve, telling him he needed to confess his sins, too. He wasn't a sinner. Well, he was living a lie right along with her, but that wasn't his fault. It was hers. He'd never done anything bad. He'd donated his time to help coach a Little League team when he'd been stationed in Washington. He never cheated on his taxes. He always behaved himself with women. What did he have to confess?

But, even as he tried to convince himself he wasn't a sinner, Trapper's words came flooding over him, and he couldn't get them out of his mind. *"God made the rules. It's up to us to decide if we want to follow them."*

"Not now, God. Not now."

❧

Jackie arose early the next morning and sorted through the things she'd be taking with her and the things she'd leave behind, placing them in piles until she could get some packing boxes. The shipping costs would be outrageous, but some things she couldn't bear to leave behind, things that meant a great deal to her. It would be worth the extra expense to keep them. Although Sam had said he'd give her a week to come clean with everyone, after thinking things over, she'd decided it would be best for everyone if she got it over with as soon as possible. It made no sense to delay it.

She worked like a madwoman at the shop, organizing shelves, setting up new displays, anything she could think of that would leave the shop in the best condition possible when the day arrived that she had to leave. She owed that much to Glorianna. Just the thought of telling her best friend in all the world that she had lied and was walking away from her made her sick to her stomach.

She was desperate now to finish the hand-quilting on the little blocks. Although tired from her busy day, after supper she began work on the twelfth block. She smiled as she placed each tiny stitch, comforted by the knowledge she was no longer in control of her life. God was. How sweet it was to commune with Him now that she'd made her peace with Him. She found herself pouring out her heart to Him, telling Him things she'd never think of telling another living soul. What a joy it was to know now that someday she'd be in heaven. If only Sam could be there with her.

The next day was much the same as the day before, with Jackie making sure she'd tied her loose ends in readiness for her departure. That evening she carried the box containing the blocks into the living room, tuned the radio to her favorite station, and worked with perseverance until she'd finished the twelfth block, sewing in her love with each stitch. Working on the quilt brought her great joy and a happiness she knew had to come from God. She even took time to write and attach the final love note to Sammy.

Jackie arrived at the shop way ahead of the staff the next morning. There were things she wanted to do without an audience. By the time the other employees arrived, she was in her office working on the final additions to the books, bringing every entry as up to date as possible. It'd been an excellent year for the shop. The books showed the profit margin had risen dramatically because of some of the new programs and classes she'd implemented. At least, as far as the shop was concerned, she could hold her head high. *Too bad I can't say the same thing about my personal life!*

Later that day she phoned Glorianna, Tina, and Emily and invited them and their husbands to her apartment the next evening for dessert, saying she had some things to tell them. She was excited about the first thing, and it would be easy to tell, that she'd accepted the Lord; but the second one, confessing her lies, was going to be extremely difficult. She wanted to invite Sam, too, but she feared his being there might make things more awkward for her and for them. No, she was the one who'd not only lied to them but convinced Sam to go along with her lies against his better judgment. She alone was the one who should tell them. Though each of the women quizzed her as to the purpose of her invitation, she held strong and kept her silence.

That evening, Jackie flitted around her apartment, cleaning and moving anything into the back bedroom that would give even a hint of her plans to leave. Once everything was in place, she took her shower and climbed into bed. She pulled the box of quilt blocks up beside her, taking them out one by one to admire them, then fanning them out across the bed. As she stared at the intricate patterns she'd quilted onto each block, quiet tears slipped down her cheeks. All twelve blocks were so beautiful, each with its own intricate pattern, and attached to each one was her love note to Sammy. She could assemble them into a quilt later by adding the sashings and borders. It'd been important to her that she have all twelve completed before she left Alaska, and she had accomplished her goal.

She'd worked on many quilts since joining the staff of the Bear Paw Quilt Shop, but none of them held the meaning of this one. She'd quilted her very heart and soul into these blocks.

Once she'd put the stack back in the box, she picked up the Bible from her nightstand and read until nearly midnight. Then, kneeling by her bed, eyes closed, hands folded, she prayed. *God, I know You've forgiven me for my sins, and I praise You for that, but I wonder if even You can get me out of this mess I've made for myself. I've not only destroyed any future I might have had here in Alaska with my lies, but I've destroyed Sam's job as well. I want to do the right thing, and I need Your help.* As she crawled into bed, a sweet peace came over her, and she slept more soundly than she had in weeks, despite the turmoil going on in her life.

Although several of the staff raised questioning brows the next day when Jackie praised them for their work and thanked them for their cooperation with her, no one questioned her motives. Since this was the final day she'd spend in the shop, she couldn't resist letting them know how important they had become to her.

When all the employees had left for the day and she was alone in the shop, she gathered up the last box of her personal belongings. She stood gazing at the array of lovely quilts mounted on the walls, the colorful rows and rows of fabric and all the other things she'd grown to love since coming to work seventeen years ago at the Bear Paw. Finally pulling herself away, she moved through the stockroom and out the heavy steel door, locking it securely behind her before climbing the steps to her apartment. She had one hour to prepare for her invited guests.

After Jackie freshened up, she arranged the little cakes she'd bought at the bakery on a lovely cut-glass tray and placed it on the table next to the bouquet of fresh flowers she'd picked up at the florist. She switched on the coffeepot, added silverware, napkins, plates, cups, and saucers to the table, then stood back to give the room one final check. Everything was ready.

Glorianna, Trapper, Tina, Hank, Emily, and Dyami arrived right on time, each one smiling at her as she took their coats and hung them in the hall closet.

"Hey, where's Sam?" Dyami asked, rubbing his hands together and looking around.

"I–I didn't invite him."

"I figured you'd invite him, too," Trapper said with a raised brow. "He's in town. We got back from Skagway this afternoon. Want me to call him?"

Jackie shook her head. "No. I purposely didn't invite him."

Although brows raised and everyone seemed surprised by her words, no one made any further comment.

"Please," Jackie said, gesturing toward the dessert table in hopes of changing the conversation, "help yourselves. I have plenty of everything."

Once everyone had been served and seated on the sofa and chairs she'd arranged in a half circle, Jackie moved to stand in front of them, her heart racing, her palms sweaty. Other than facing Sam after she'd lost the baby, this was the hardest thing she'd ever had to do.

"Okay, out with it," Glorianna said, looking somewhat worried. "Please don't tell me someone has made you a better offer and you're quitting your job."

Emily gave Glorianna a knowing grin. "If her news is what I think it is, you'll be happy to hear it!"

Glorianna planted her hands on her hips with a playful

smile toward her mother-in-law. "She's told you, and she hasn't told me? I thought I was Jackie's best friend!"

"Emily's right. Part of my news is good, and it's one of the reasons I called all of you here tonight." Jackie tried to push the bad news to the back of her mind and gave them a joyous smile of victory. "Emily came to see me the other night. After we talked and she explained a few things to me, I accepted the Lord as my Savior!"

Glorianna and Tina rushed to her side, congratulating her and hugging her so tightly it was hard for her to breathe.

"That's the best news I've heard in a long time," Trapper said, his own joy radiating from his bearded face.

"Tina and I have been praying for you every day," Hank added, grinning.

Jackie smiled at each one in the circle. These people had been her family. They'd encouraged her, come to her aid whenever she'd needed them. "I–I know I should've done it a long time ago, but I was trying to make things too hard. When sweet Emily made me see how simple God's plan really is and convinced me He could love someone like me, I had no other choice but to ask Him to take over my life."

"Well, I'm glad you invited us all here. This is a cause for celebration." Trapper rose and moved to the table, refilling his cup and picking up another little cake. "Anyone else for a refill?"

Once everyone had refilled their cups and added another cake to their plates, they seated themselves again, and Jackie stood before them. The lump in her throat was nearly gagging her to silence, and she wondered if she'd be able to get the words out—words she'd rehearsed so carefully all day.

"Please, everyone. I–I have something else to tell you. Some–something that must be said."

nine

All chatter stopped as six people gave her their full attention. She was sure her voice reflected the panic going on inside her.

"What I'm about to tell you will shock you, but I'm hoping you'll hear me out." She clenched her fists at her sides and drew in a deep breath.

"I've lied to everyone from the first day I walked into the Bear Paw and applied for a job. I told everyone I was a widow and that my husband died in a hunting accident. He didn't. He divorced me."

"You've lied to me all this time, Jackie? Why? I don't understand."

"It started out with my lie to Anna when she hired me. She mentioned that the girl whose place I would be taking had been divorced during the time she worked at the Bear Paw, and Anna had been very upset by it and had expressed her feelings to the girl. That was the reason the girl had quit. I knew, right then, if she found out I had just gone through a divorce she wouldn't hire me, so I told her I was a widow. I needed that job. By the time you inherited the quilt shop from Anna, the lie had become a solid part of my life. There was no way for me to unravel it. I knew I had to live with it. You were as adamant as Anna about divorce. I knew I couldn't tell you, either."

"You're right concerning Anna's feelings about divorce," Emily said with a sympathetic smile toward Jackie. "She was almost glad when that girl left. She had strong feelings about those who broke their marriage vows, and she made no bones about expressing those feelings openly and at every opportunity."

"There's more," Jackie said, holding up her hand. "Please let me finish."

Glorianna nodded and settled back in her chair.

"My husband was nearly four years older than me. We married right after I graduated from high school, and he joined the army." She paused, remembering that happy time. "Everything was great the first three years. I loved him with all my heart, and I think he loved me the same way. Then—"

Trapper stood and gave her a compassionate smile. "Jackie, you really don't have to tell us this. It's obvious you're very emotional about your marriage and the divorce, but your business is your business."

"No, it's not. All of you deserve to know, especially Glorianna. Oh, I know she'll never be able to trust me to work at the shop again, now that I've told you the truth and she knows she's had a divorced liar working for her; but the time has come that I have to make things right. Not only with you six, but with God." She motioned Trapper back down to his seat. "Please, Trapper. I have to tell you the complete story. You'll see why later."

Although he seemed reluctant, Trapper settled back in the chair and waited.

"I'd been working at a fast-food place trying to get enough money saved so I could go to college. Then one day, out of the blue, my husband came home from a training trip and told me he wanted us to have a baby as soon as possible. Just like that. We'd never even discussed when we'd start a family, just that someday we would! I'd always talked about wanting to go to college and making something of myself. I was from a poor, uneducated family, and I was determined to have a career." As she grabbed onto the back of Emily's chair for support, she felt the woman's hand cup over hers, and Jackie gave Emily a smile.

"I was furious with him. I tried to explain to him that I hadn't even thought of having children yet and how badly I wanted to have a career, but he was adamant. He said if I loved him I'd give him a baby, and he accused me of being selfish."

She looked around and found six faces staring at her. She couldn't help but wonder what was going on in their minds.

"We argued about it nearly every day, but neither of us would give in. My girlfriends sided with me and told me I had every right to have a career. After all, he did! His army buddies sided with him, many of them saying they'd insisted their wives give up any idea of having a career to become mothers. Oh, I think we both still loved one another. I know I loved him, and we expressed our love often, but that didn't stop the fighting over the issue." She paused to gather her thoughts. *Be honest. Tell them the whole story, exactly as it happened. No lies. No excuses.*

"Then the thing I least expected happened. The base doctor told me I was pregnant. I was furious, but my husband was ecstatic. He rushed out and began buying all sorts of baby things, spending money we didn't have, for the baby I didn't want. I–I told him—" She stopped midsentence. How could she say the words?

"I–I told him—I was going to have an—an abortion."

A unified gasp came from the group, and Jackie could tell by their expressions her declaration had shocked them beyond belief.

"Needless to say, he was livid. He swore at me and called me terrible names and said if I went through with it I would be a murderer! I tried to explain my feelings to him, but he wouldn't listen. Two of my girlfriends, who hadn't wanted children but whose husbands had, had gone through abortions, one twice, and they encouraged me to stand up to him. They told me to remind him this was my body, not his, that we were talking about. The decision should be mine."

She paused and thought her words over carefully before going on.

"I hated being pregnant. I couldn't keep anything down and had to quit my job, which infuriated me. I struggled along for nearly three more months, knowing if I was to have an abortion it'd have to be soon. He went to every doctor's appointment with me and acted like a sappy new father, asking the poor doctor all sorts of questions. I didn't want him to go, but he insisted. Then, a couple of weeks after my fourth month checkup, he came home all excited because the army was sending him on a special mission to Germany. My first thought was that with him gone it'd be easier to arrange an abortion. I'd gained way too much weight, my hands and feet were swollen, and even my nose had gotten bigger. All I could think about was getting rid of that baby and getting back to my normal self and how mad I was at my husband for leaving me alone at a time like this."

Even though no one voiced a comment, she could tell from their expressions that her friends were in shock, and she could almost hear their thoughts. Jackie? This Jackie they'd known so well? Never!

"The day my husband left, we had the worst fight of all. It went on most of the day while he was packing. His final words to me as he left the house, knowing it would be at least two months before he got back, were 'If you do anything to get rid of that baby while I'm gone, I'll divorce you!' and I had no doubt he meant it. But his threats didn't matter. I was so arrogant and immature I'd already decided what I did with that baby was my business, not his. I–I fully intended to get rid of it, but a few weeks later, something happened that I hadn't counted on. I was sitting in a chair watching TV when I felt something. A movement in my stomach. As I rubbed my hand over the spot, I felt it again. I can't begin to tell you what a sensation that was. For the first time, I realized that *thing* in my stomach, the *thing* I wanted to rid myself of, wasn't a *thing* at all. It was a live human being! I sat in awe as my baby moved! *My* baby!"

Jackie cast a quick glance toward Glorianna and found the woman's eyes as round as saucers.

"I called and excitedly told the base doctor the next morning about the movement, and you know what he said? 'That little one wanted his mommy to know he was doing fine.' I called my girlfriends and told them I'd decided against the abortion. They told me I was a fool, but I didn't care. I went to my appointment that next week, and when I heard my baby's heartbeat I broke down and cried. I was so happy. Because I was still spotting, the doctor wanted to do an ultrasound immediately, to make sure everything was okay."

Tina's hand spread across her stomach. "Oh, Jackie, what an ordeal for both of you."

"Wh–when"—Jackie gulped in a breath of air as she felt a tear roll down her cheek—"wh–when I actually saw my baby on that screen, I screamed out with joy and wondered how I could ever have considered getting rid of our precious baby. The doctor told me our baby was a boy. I was so happy."

She paused to catch another breath. "But the doctor's face

told me something was wrong. When I asked him about it, he said the next few weeks would be critical and mentioned something about low-lying placenta previa, which I didn't understand. He said I'd have to stay in bed and be very careful. By that time, I wanted that baby so bad, I would've gone to the moon if the doctor had asked me."

"Did you tell your husband?" Tina asked timidly, as if she was afraid her question might upset Jackie.

"I wanted to. I hadn't heard from him since he'd left, which kind of surprised me. But, I guess, knowing the way I felt, he figured it'd be best to leave me alone. He knew my mind had been made up, and I suppose he figured he'd done everything he could to stop me from going through with the abortion. I tried to call him at the base. I was so happy, and I wanted him to be happy, too. I even called his commander. He said my husband was out on maneuvers and couldn't be reached, unless it was an emergency."

She paused long enough to take a sip of her cold coffee, then went on. "I contacted a few of his buddies that evening and told them to have him call me if they heard from him, but he never did."

"But things went along okay?" Glorianna asked, leaning forward, a tender look on her face now.

"Actually, I felt better than I had in months. I was no longer sick to my stomach, and the swelling in my feet and hands had stopped. My neighbor, bless her heart, did my grocery shopping and cooked me a few meals. I was marking the days off on the calendar until my son would arrive and I could hold him in my arms. I was so sure things between my husband and me would return to normal once he learned I was as excited as he was about the birth of our precious baby."

"Was he?" Emily asked, her eyes wide.

"I never had a chance to find out. The day before my next doctor's appointment, I began to hemorrhage. Terrified, I grabbed my car keys and headed for the hospital."

Am I telling them more than they need to know? she wondered as she regrouped her thoughts, her misty gaze flitting from one person to the next.

"I ran into the emergency room screaming for someone to help me, but there was nothing they could do." She fought to hold back her tears, but the memory was too much. "Our baby was stillborn, which the doctor said meant if there hadn't been any trouble, he was old enough that he could have survived outside the womb."

Glorianna rushed to her side and cradled her in her arms. "Oh, Jackie—I'm so sorry. I had no idea, and to think you were all alone when it happened."

"I–I've never felt so all alone. I needed my husband there with me."

The room took on an eerie silence.

After Glorianna went back to her chair and Jackie regained her composure, she continued. "They kept me overnight, I think because I was so despondent. One of the social workers came to talk to me about losing my baby; then she drove me home in her car while a friend of hers followed in my car. Two days later, my husband got back from his mission."

"He had to be upset by your baby's death, but he must've been glad to hear you'd had a change of heart," Trapper said, leaning forward.

"He didn't believe I'd miscarried. He was outraged when I tried to tell him our baby's death hadn't been my fault. He accused me of lying, saying I'd been responsible for our baby's death. His words hurt, but after the way I'd been so insistent about not wanting a baby, I couldn't blame him. He—He—"

Even after all this time, Jackie found it hard to say the words. Finally, she blurted out hysterically, "He accused me of killing my own baby, then walked right out that door and went to a divorce lawyer. I never even had a chance to tell him how I'd felt our baby move and heard the heartbeat and watched it on the ultrasound screen. He didn't even know our baby was a boy."

The room was silent as all of them kept their eyes fixed on her. Jackie pulled a paper napkin from the table and dabbed at her eyes before going on.

"The day the divorce became final, I left town. I took the first bus heading out and ended up in Denver. I checked into a motel, not sure where I would go from there or what to do with my life." She hung her head, her words barely audible. "I–I even considered suicide."

When no one spoke, she swallowed hard and began again.

"Th–there was an ad in the Denver paper, advertising a cruise to Alaska. I took some of the settlement money from the divorce and booked the trip. Two weeks later, when the ship anchored in Juneau, I got off with the other passengers, intending to spend the day visiting the shops and aimlessly wandering the streets. Eventually, I ended up at the Bear Paw. When I saw a help-wanted sign in the window, I went in and applied. And, as you know, Anna hired me, and I've been here ever since."

"But I don't understand, Jackie," Glorianna said, shaking her head. "Why are you telling us this now? Why didn't you leave your past in the past and keep your lies buried? We may never have found out, if you hadn't told us. Why resurrect old memories now?"

"Did you ever hear from your husband again?" Tina asked, ignoring Glorianna's question.

"Not until recently. I'd cut all ties with my past and didn't expect to hear from him ever again. I supposed he'd married someone else and, by now, had a houseful of the kids he'd wanted."

"You've heard from him?" Hank asked as he slipped his arm about his wife and pulled her close. "I can't imagine any husband being that cruel."

Jackie weighed her words carefully. Her intent wasn't to make Sam look bad. "Yes, I've heard from him, but please don't judge him too harshly. You have to remember how badly he wanted that baby. I was the one who said I was going to get an abortion. Of course he was going to be upset. I can see that now. At the time, I felt he was being ridiculous. I was the one who listened to my friends' bad advice. We were both wrong."

"Does he want to make things right? Is that why you've heard from him?"

Jackie shook her head sadly. "No, Glorianna. I wish that was the reason. He didn't have any idea I was in Juneau, until the two of us ended up at the same place at the same time. He's the reason I've never married or been interested in dating another man. I still love him and always will."

"How does he feel about you?"

"Oh, Tina, I have no idea. He still says he could never live with me after I purposely lost our baby, so I assume he no longer has any feelings for me. I've tried to tell him the truth—that although I did everything the doctor told me, I miscarried—but he won't even discuss it. He doesn't believe a word I say."

"I'd like to meet that guy," Trapper said, shaking his head. "Having a baby should be the decision of both the husband *and* the wife. No man has a right to dictate to his wife, especially when it involves her body. Is he still here in Juneau?"

Jackie nodded. "Yes, Trapper. It's Sam."

ten

Trapper leaped to his feet. "Sam? Sam Mulvaney? Surely not! Is this some kind of a joke?"

The overwhelming silence in the room was deafening.

Jackie shook her head sadly while trying to keep her emotions in check. "No, no joke. Sam is my ex-husband, my baby's father."

"But I'm the one who talked him into coming here!" Trapper reasoned aloud. "He told me he'd been divorced, but he never mentioned a baby."

Tina's hand went to her mouth. "And to think Glorianna and I tried to match the two of you up! We thought you were perfect for one another."

"I'm still confused." Trapper rubbed at his forehead. "If what you're telling us is true, and I have no reason to believe it's anything but the truth, that means Sam has been deceiving us, too. But why?"

"Don't blame Sam. I asked him to lie for me," Jackie confessed. "He didn't want to; in fact, he refused. But I knew when Glorianna found out I'd been lying about my past she wouldn't let me keep working at the shop. So when I ran into Sam in the parking lot the first night he came to Alaska—"

"That's the first time you'd seen him since your divorce?"

Jackie gave Tina a weak smile. "Yes, that's the reason we were both a bit late. We had a long talk before we came into the Grizzly Bear. After much persuasion, I was able to convince Sam to keep my secret, but he made me promise, if the truth ever came out, I would take full responsibility. That's what I'm trying to do now."

Hank shook his head. "I can't believe it. Sam Mulvaney."

"That's why he later resigned and headed back to Memphis," Jackie explained. "He couldn't stand deceiving you, Trapper."

Glorianna flinched. "And I arranged for the two of you to be booked on the same flight to Seattle and have reservations at the same hotel."

"You had no idea, Glorianna. You meant well. In fact, Sam and I talked about the matchmaking you and Tina were trying to do."

"No wonder you didn't invite Sam to be here tonight," Dyami said, picking up his cup and refilling it.

"So I'm leaving Alaska. I have reservations on a late afternoon flight tomorrow." She turned to Glorianna. "I've done the best I could to make sure the shop is in order. You'll find all the book work up to date, and I've made sure all the supplies are ordered. I'll leave the shop keys, as well as the keys to my apartment, on the table when I leave."

"Maybe we'd better talk about this—"

Jackie shook her head. "No, Glorianna. I know how important honesty is to you in everything. You'd never be able to trust me again, knowing how I've lied to you." Then turning to the others she said, "I want all of you to know how much you've meant to me. I love each one of you and hope you can find it in your heart, someday, to forgive me."

"Is—is Sam going with you?" Trapper asked.

She gave him a nervous laugh. "No, I'm afraid where I go

and what I do is the last thing Sam is interested in. He's made it perfectly clear he wants nothing more to do with me."

"Then he's staying?" Glorianna asked.

Jackie shrugged. "I doubt it. He's convinced Trapper won't want a liar as a partner, but I'm sure he'll let you know." She moved from one to another, giving them each a guarded hug. "Please pray for me, and be assured I'll be praying for you. Accepting the Lord was worth coming to Alaska. Now, if you'll excuse me, I have some things to finish up if I'm going to make my flight tomorrow."

Her six guests filed out without a word, each wearing a stunned expression that broke her heart. After locking the door behind them, Jackie washed and dried the dishes, making sure each one was put in its place. She was determined to leave the apartment as clean as she'd found it when she'd moved in.

Exhausted from the experience of having to confess her lies, after praying and thanking God for giving her the strength to tell them the truth, Jackie fell into bed, worn out both physically and mentally.

After a night of tossing and turning, she crawled out of bed at five. Although most of her things were already packed, she still had much to do. She scurried around the apartment—dusting, running the sweeper, cleaning windows and mirrors—and carried a few boxes and an odd assortment of things that needed to be boxed into the living room and placed them on the floor. By nine o'clock, she had nearly everything in order. Gathering a few large boxes from the quilt shop storeroom to hold the things she'd decided to ship was the only task that remained. *I can't do that!* she realized suddenly. *Do I really want to go into that storeroom and take a chance on running into some of the staff and having to explain my reasons for leaving?* Then she remembered the Dumpsters out behind the big grocery store down past the courthouse. *They probably have exactly what I need.*

She shoved a few of the smaller boxes to one side, picked up her purse and keys, and quickly made her way down the stairs to her car.

❧

Sam sat eyeing the phone. He'd told Jackie he'd give her one week and if she didn't tell Glorianna and Trapper the truth by then, he was going to tell them. Surely she'd alert him before she admitted to them her life had been a lie.

He glanced at his watch. *I'm going that way. Maybe I'll stop by the quilt shop and ask her if she's decided when she's going to tell them. She's probably there by now.*

"No, she's not here yet," one of the clerks told him when he entered through the back way. "That's funny, too, because she's always the first one here. I hope she's not sick."

Sam excused himself and raced up the outside stairway, taking two steps at a time. He knocked, but when she didn't respond he tried the door. Finding it standing slightly ajar, he ventured in, calling out her name. Boxes were piled near the door and some by her chair. Others that looked as if they were ready to be packed sat on the sofa, the chairs, and the coffee table. No doubt about it—Jackie was preparing to leave Juneau.

Noticing the red light was glowing on the coffeepot, he took a cup from the cupboard and filled it, picked up one of the little cakes sitting on a plate in the middle of the table, then sat down in the recliner to wait for her return. She must have planned to come back soon since the coffeepot was still turned on and the door was unlocked. Maybe she was visiting with a neighbor or had run to the store for something.

Sam sipped the hot coffee slowly, listening carefully for any sounds of her return. He pulled a magazine from the wastebasket sitting next to the chair and leafed through it. Finding nothing of interest, he leaned to put it back where he'd found it when he noticed a white box sitting on the floor near his feet. Deciding it was probably some quilting thing Jackie was working on, and having nothing better to do, he pulled out the little stack of blocks and placed them on his knee. He gazed at the intricate, hand-quilted design on the top one and was amazed at the evenness of the stitches and how tiny they were. The woman was a masterful quilter, no doubt about it.

As he started to place it back on the pile, he noticed a note pinned to the back. Carefully he unpinned the paper, unfolded it, and began to read: *Dear Sammy, I don't know why I'm writing this, except to say I love you and to remind you—you are in my thoughts day and night.*

Sam's brows rose. "I thought she told me she never had a serious boyfriend. Who is Sammy?" he asked aloud.

His interest piqued, he picked up the second block.

Sammy, my dear, facing up to the fact that you were gone was the hardest thing I've ever had to do. I'm making this quilt for you, Sammy. Of course you'll never see it, but I'm making it as a token of my love. Don't think too harshly of me. Please.

He picked up the third block and quickly flipped it over. "Another note?"

My precious one. I wish you were here with me. I'm miserable without you. I want so much to hold you in my arms and kiss your sweet face. I cry as I go to bed each night, wishing I could hug you to me.

"He left her? When? And why is she making a quilt for someone who must've walked out on her?"

He removed the pin from the fourth block, being careful not to tear the paper. *My beloved one. I miss you desperately. If only I could hold you and kiss your dear face. You're constantly on my mind. Where are you now, Sweetheart? In a better place? A place filled with love and sunshine? I long to be with you.*

Sam stared at the note. "Who is this Sammy character?" He pinned the notes back where they belonged and pulled out the next block, noting it too was hand-quilted with beautiful, even stitches. As he suspected, a note was pinned to it as well.

I pulled out your pictures today. You looked so handsome in that cap. Just looking at it made me smile. The day those pictures were taken will be etched into my memory forever, especially the one taken of us in the rocking chair.

He hurriedly grabbed up the sixth block. *I have your birthday circled on the calendar, my love. Every year on your special day I buy a little cake and light a candle. If only I could spend those days with you. The pain of losing you never goes away.*

Sam scratched his head. More confused by her words than ever, he replaced the pin and picked up the seventh block. "Who is this guy?"

He pricked his finger as he struggled with the tiny safety pin. After grabbing his handkerchief and blotting his finger, he read the note.

Sammy, my love, my precious one. Today something unexpected happened. I ran into Sam! Yes, Sam. He's in Alaska. I wanted to talk to him about you, but I couldn't. He'd never understand, and I didn't want to argue. I've made a new life for myself here. I don't want it spoiled. He made it quite clear years ago he wanted nothing to do with me, and it broke my heart. I've decided this uilt will be my tribute to you, Sammy, darling. I wish I could ive it to you.

"This doesn't make any sense. Why would she mention me, nd why is she making a quilt as a tribute to him? Did he die n a car accident or from some disease?" He read on out of heer curiosity.

If only Sam had believed me, dear Sammy, perhaps things would have turned out differently. I've heard stress does strange hings to your body, and I was certainly under a great deal of tress when I was carrying you. Oh, I admit I didn't want you when your daddy first talked about having a baby. But the day I elt you move—well, it was a miracle, Sammy. All of a sudden I aw you as a real baby, and I shouted out with joy. I wish Sam ould've been there with us. It was an awesome experience.

Sam let out a gasp, and his hands began to tremble. "Sammy vas our baby?" He stared at the words. "How can that be?"

Then the doctor let me listen to your heartbeat, and I've never elt such happiness. My baby! The day he did the ultrasound was he most exciting day of my life. I actually got to see you! Not veryone would have thought so, but to me you were beautiful. I lecided at that very moment to name you Sammy, after your ather. If only Sam had been there with me, my joy would have een complete. I tried to phone him, to tell him about you, but he was on that mission to Germany and couldn't be reached. Oh, Sammy, I loved him so much. If only your father had loved me nough to trust me and believe me.

Sam stared at the paper, his hands still shaking. Had Jackie een telling him the truth?

I'm so afraid you experienced pain. I keep thinking there nust've been something I could've done differently, even though I now now I couldn't. It's just that I'm your mommy, Sammy, and I was supposed to take care of you. There was nothing I could do but lie there and watch it happen and know I couldn't stop it. I tried so hard to do the right things for you from the day I felt you move inside me. I ate healthy foods, exercised, everything I knew to do; but it wasn't good enough. I wanted to protect you, to keep you safe—to give you the best start in life I could. Where did I fail you, my precious one? My darling child? Sam clutched the note to his chest as his eyes filled with tears. "Oh, Jackie, if you were telling me the truth, I've done you a terrible injustice."

He took a deep breath and read on. *I'm so sad tonight, Sammy. Your father decided he couldn't keep lying to everyone. He's going to resign from his partnership with Trapper and go back to Memphis. Although his being here has made my life difficult, I didn't want him to go. I still love him. I always will.*

Sam buried his head in his hands. "Oh, Jackie, how could I have treated you like that? I loved you, too!"

The eighth block tore at his heart. *Oh, Sammy, guess what! Your father is back in Juneau. Although he's been gone only a few days, I've missed him terribly. Today he almost treated me like I was human. We've reached an agreement. We're going to try to be friends. Maybe he's finally beginning to realize I've told him the truth all along!*

Sam smiled as he remembered that day. Jackie had never looked more beautiful as she'd grinned at him over her shopping cart. He'd never admit it to her, but in his heart, although he knew it was impossible, he had wished their relationship could be more than just friends.

"Oh, Jackie, it seems since we've found each other again, our lives have been nothing but a roller coaster of emotions. I'm sorry for taking you on this crazy ride going nowhere."

He pulled the next block from the stack and unpinned its note.

It's late, and I'm tired; but before going to bed I had to write and tell you how much I love you. Sometimes I dream of holding you and kissing your sweet face, only to wake up and find I'm alone in my room. It's hard for me to realize you've been gone this long. Life has been hard without you, Sammy. Very hard. I only wish your father would accept the truth.

Glorianna told me some disturbing things a few days ago. She said if I don't confess my sins and ask God to forgive them, I can't go to heaven. I can't get her words out of my head. I guess I'm going to have to read the Bible for myself. If you were here with me, perhaps we could read it together. It makes me sad I was never able to read those sweet little children's storybooks to you at bedtime. I love you, Baby.

Sam swallowed hard and rubbed at his eyes, the words blurring on the paper. Trapper had told him the same thing Glorianna had told Jackie. Could God really be that judgmental?

Oh, Sammy, your father kissed me, the note on the tenth block said. *Although later he said it'd been a mistake. But I knew better. He wanted to kiss me. I could tell. Could he still have feelings for me? Unfortunately, we got into another argument afterward, and we ended up coming back from Seattle separately. I'm so confused by his actions. He admitted he is still drawn to me. Why can't he believe me? If only he'd talked to the doctor, checked the emergency room records; then he'd have known I was telling the truth.*

Sam stared at the paper, then smacked the side of his head with his palm. Why hadn't he bothered to check the hospital records? "Why? Because I was too stubborn, that's why! I was so sure she'd done what she'd threatened to do that I wouldn't even listen to her." His gaze went back to the paper, and he reread the words: *If only he'd talked to the doctor, checked the emergency room records; then he'd have known I was telling the truth.*

He stared at the words, rereading them again. "Why didn't I listen to her? Give her a chance to prove she was telling the truth after all? I never once considered what she was going through. She was young, naïve, with no desire to have a baby at that time, and I insisted on it. Having a baby should've been *our* decision, not just mine. How could I have been so selfish?"

He sat for a long time, staring at the wall, remembering the many arguments they'd had—most of them started by him. "If only I had a chance to go back, how differently I'd do things."

With a deep sigh, he unpinned the note from the eleventh block.

Oh, Sammy, I saw your father today. We all went to church, but I made sure to sit on the opposite end of the pew. The words the pastor read from the Bible about lying lips really got to me. I'm sure God is upset with me. It seems my life is built on nothing but lies.

But something good came of it, my dear one. Thinking I was sick, dear Emily Timberwolf came to see me and brought me some soup. She's such a kind and caring woman. She told me, straight out, I needed to get my life right with God—that God wanted to forgive my sins—that He was a God of love. And, Sammy, guess what! I did it! Right here in this very apartment. I can't begin to tell you of the sweet peace that came over me. Now I know I'll be in heaven someday. If only Sam could be there with me.

Sam gulped hard as his fingers rubbed at his eyes and the words on the paper blurred. His heart raced as he tried to catch his breath. "Emily Timberwolf? She must've told Jackie the same thing Trapper told me. That God wants to forgive my sins, but first I have to admit I'm a sinner." He shook his head sadly. "Who did I think I was kidding? I am a sinner. If I'd done nothing worse in my life than what I've done to Jackie, the woman who at one time I loved more than life itself, I'm sure God would see me as a terrible sinner! Oh, God, what have I done? What have I done?"

He leaned back in the chair, trying to gather some semblance of composure, his gut tied in knots. *If only Sam could be there with me.* Her words rang in his ears. "After all I've done to her, she still wants us to be together." Finally, he lifted the note and continued to read.

I was so happy knowing God loved me and could forgive me, but my joy soon turned to sadness, Sammy. Your father came to me and said he couldn't go on with our lying. I tried to tell him I'd gotten my life straightened out with God and He'd forgiven me, but he didn't seem to care. He was more interested in the ultimatum he was giving me.

Sam paused and blotted at his eyes with his sleeve.

Either I tell Trapper and Glorianna, or he will. He's right. I know he is. This lying is killing me, too. He's given me a few days to get things ready to leave before I have to tell them. After that, I'll be flying out of Juneau and away from the friends I love. But at least I won't have to keep living a lie. Oh, Sammy, if only you'd lived, our little family might be together now, and none of this lying would have happened.

Carefully, Sam repinned the paper to the back of the eleventh block, again taking note of the tiny stitches his ex-wife had lovingly added, each one perfectly in line with the one before it. He could almost see her sweet face as she painstakingly wove the needle in and out of the fabric.

The sound of a car's engine sent him quickly to the window, but it was only the next-door neighbor. He refilled his coffee cup and stood staring at the white box for a long time before he got up the courage to sit back down and pick up the last block, knowing how upset Jackie would be if she knew he was delving into her personal items like this. It was obvious she had never intended for anyone but her to see the blocks or read the notes she had penned to her son.

Finally, he settled back down in the chair, looked over the block, and unpinned its note.

Quilting this twelfth block and writing this note, my dear baby, has brought back bittersweet memories. I'm so thankful, even though the doctor was afraid to let me see you, that he finally agreed and allowed me to hold you close to my heart and kiss you good-bye. Other than the day I said 'I do' to your father, those were the most precious moments of my life.

You looked so sweet as you lay in my arms, swaddled in that pale blue blanket with that funny little hat on your head as the nurse took our picture. I've cherished those little pictures, Sammy. Those first few years I kept them locked away in my diary. Just the sight of them made me burst uncontrollably into tears. But things have changed since that awful time of my life. I've grown up, Sammy. I've matured. Now I love to hold your pictures next to my heart and remember your sweet little innocent face. Someday maybe I'll be able to look at the picture my friend took of your tiny gravestone.

Gravestone! The word yanked Sam back to reality. He leaned his head against the back of the chair and closed his eyes. "My son is buried somewhere in the cold, cold ground, and I don't even know where?"

I was hoping one day, her note went on, *your father would want to see the pictures I've saved.*

"Why should she want to show them to me after the hurt I've caused her? I failed my wife when she needed me most."

His head swirled. "Dear God, what You must think of me, too. How could either You or Jackie ever forgive me?" he cried aloud.

Trapper's words penetrated his thoughts. *"So many people turn their backs on God's Son, Sam. Don't be one of them."*

Sam lifted his tear-filled eyes heavenward. "But I am one of them, God! I've not only turned my back on *Your* Son, but I've turned my back on *my* own son as well and on my wife, too. Can You ever forgive me? Can Jackie ever forgive me?"

As Sam stared upward, he remembered one of the Scripture verses about forgiveness he'd heard at Trapper's church—that if you confess your sins and ask forgiveness, God will do it.

"Can it be that simple, Lord?" he asked out loud, his voice low and wavering. "If I do as Your Word says, can I know for sure I'm going to heaven?"

Another verse from the Bible filled his mind as clearly as if the pastor were standing beside him now, reading it to him. *" 'Whosoever believeth in him should not perish, but have eternal life.' " I want to go to heaven, God. Surely, if You said it, it's true.* He longed to have that same peace Jackie spoke about when she'd told him her good news.

Pulling a handkerchief from his hip pocket, he wiped it across his eyes before glancing at the wall clock. He'd been there for nearly forty-five minutes. Where was Jackie?

He paced about the room, trying to imagine the gamut of emotions Jackie must have felt as she worked on those quilt blocks and wrote her notes to her baby. *Their* baby. Finally, he moved back to the chair, picked up the last note again, and read the rest of the words.

I'm sad today, my precious Sammy. Your father said some very cruel things to me before he left for Skagway. If only he'd been there when I miscarried you and witnessed my sorrow, he'd know I could never harm you. I'm afraid he'll go to his grave believing I ended your life willingly. I've turned this all over to God now, Baby. It's in His hands. No matter what happens or how much Sam's dreadful accusations hurt me, I'll always love your father. And I'll always love you.

With all my love, Mama.

The paper fell to the floor as Sam thrust his head into his hands and wept. "Oh, God," he cried out from the depths of his soul, "I've sinned against You so many times in so many ways. Please, please forgive me for ever denying I'm a sinner." He dropped to his knees and spread his arms open wide, lifting his face upward. "Forgive me, I pray. I believe what You said in the Bible. I'm asking You to come into my heart and cleanse it. I'm not worthy of Your love, but I beg You to hear me now. Take me, God. I'm giving myself totally to You. I've made such a mess of my life. Only You can straighten it out."

Sam froze at the sound of the door opening behind him. He'd been so caught up in communing with God that he hadn't heard someone coming up the outside stairway. He cast a hurried, concerned glance at the pile of quilt blocks he'd left on the floor.

"Sam? What are you doing here?" Jackie glared at him as she pushed the door closed behind her, shutting out the cold morning chill.

eleven

Her words hung in the air like icicles from a roof, unanswered, as Sam stared at her. "I–I—" His gaze went to the paper lying on the floor at his feet.

Jackie followed his gaze, then gasped as she quickly bent to retrieve the paper. "You—you've been—"

He nodded. "Yes, I know I had no right, but—"

"How could you? These letters are to my son! Surely they were of no interest to you! Did you have to spoil the one thing I had left? How dare you invade my privacy?"

Sam struggled for the right words. "Th–the door. It was standing slightly open."

"No, I distinctly remember turning the lock." She gathered up the quilt blocks, placed the note on top of them, and stuffed them hurriedly into the white box.

He stood, his hands dangling idly at his sides, like a penitent child who'd run out of excuses for his errant behavior. "I–I know you don't believe me, Jackie, but the door was standing open. You know I don't have a key."

A bit of the harsh anger disappeared from her face as she eyed the door and gave him an exasperated look. "I do have to tug on it sometimes to get the lock to engage, but that's no excuse for you to come in here uninvited. This is my home, or at least it is until I leave for the airport this afternoon."

She snatched the box from the floor, placed it on the sofa,

and plopped down beside it, carefully replacing the lid. "I hope you didn't—"

Sam found it difficult to get his feet to move as he stood awkwardly by the chair. "I did, Jackie," he confessed, his eyes once more glazing over with tears. "I–I read them all."

She bowed her head and buried her face in her hands. "Oh, Sam. Wh–why did you have to co–come barging back into my li–life?"

He wanted so much to take her in his arms, comfort her, tell her how sorry he was, but why would she let him? So far everything he'd done since he'd come to Juneau had either blown up in his face or hurt Jackie. All because he'd been too stubborn to accept the truth. Cautiously, he moved the last few steps separating them and knelt before her, pulling her hands away from her face and taking them into his. "I'm sorry, Jackie, for everything. I–I want you to know that."

Tenderly, he kissed her fingertips one by one as he stared up into her lovely face, tears now rolling down his cheeks unashamedly. "I've sinned against you by not believing you. You were my wife! The one person in this world I loved the most and should trust the most. How could I not believe you?"

Jackie eyed him suspiciously. "I–I don't understand."

His finger pointed to the white box. "I–I read all about it, Sweetheart. How you'd decided to go through with the abortion, despite my warning." He gulped hard, barely able to say the words. "Ho–how you changed your mind when you felt our baby move inside you."

"Sam, I know you don't believe I could have a change of heart over something that sounds so simple, but"—she leaned her head back and stared at the ceiling before going on—"to me, our baby moving like that was a miracle!"

"I–I should have been there with you."

She blinked and said in a mere whisper, "Yes, you should have. You missed a wonderful experience."

"I know, and I'll never forgive myself. I could've turned down that assignment, but I was furious with you. You were determined to go through with the abortion, and I didn't want to be around when you did it. It seemed I was the only one who wanted that baby."

Her breath hitched. "I–I wanted him, too, Sam. When I felt that first movement and realized my baby was alive in me—well, all I can say is, in that moment, I became that child's mother. Me. Jackie Mulvaney."

Those two words sent daggers into his heart. Jackie Mulvaney. His wife. The one he'd promised to love, honor, and cherish. He'd vowed to protect her. From whom? If she needed protection from anyone, it was from him, her own husband!

Unsure how to proceed, Sam slowly slipped his arms about her waist and, when she didn't protest, pulled her close. "I am so sorry, Jackie, so sorry! Although I don't deserve it, I'm asking your forgiveness. Please, Sweetheart, can you find it in your heart to forgive me?"

She leaned forward with a heavy sigh, and their foreheads touched. "Forgive you for what, Sam? For the many times you accused me of killing our baby? For you coming to Alaska and ruining the life I had here with the only true friends I've ever known?" Her voice was shaky and raw with emotion.

To his dying day Sam would remember the anguish in her voice. "Yes," he answered, trying to keep his own emotions under control. "Both of those and a whole lot more. I know I don't have the right to ask for forgiveness, but I'm begging you, Sweetheart, please—try to find it in your heart to forgive me."

She drew back a bit and gave him a puzzled look. "Why do you keep calling me 'sweetheart'? I don't understand, Sam. Is this another one of your mixed signals?"

She seemed vulnerable, almost childlike herself, and suddenly, Sam's heart overflowed with love for this woman. A love he'd deigned to forget for the past seventeen years. "It's—it's because—I love you, Jackie. I always have. I guess that's why it hurt so much when you said you were going to do away with our baby. It was like you wanted to get rid of a part of me, too."

❧

Her entire being shuddered at his remark. "No! It wasn't that way at all! I"—she bowed her head shyly—"I loved you. You were my life."

"You were my life, too. I wanted us to have that baby as a symbol of our love, the two of us made into one. It nearly killed me when you—"

She put a quick finger to his lips. "Don't say it, Sam. Please."

"I know now you could never have had an abortion. Those sweet letters you wrote to our Sammy were—"

"You did read them!"

"Yes, every word. I told you I did. But only because I had to know the truth." He shifted on his heels and pulled her close. "I wish I could do something to make up for all the pain I've caused you. I'm so sorry."

The tenderness and compassion she could see in his eyes touched her deeply. Her voice a mere whisper, she told him, "All I've ever wanted was for you to believe me."

He took one of her hands and folded it in his. "I do believe you, Dearest. I've been such a fool."

Dare she believe him? Dare she trust her heart?

"God has forgiven me, Jackie, and I'm asking you to do the same thing. I want to start the rest of my life with a clean slate. Can you find it—?"

She raised her eyes and met his gaze head-on. "You did? You really asked for God's forgiveness? You're not just saying that?"

He brought up his hands to capture her face. "Yes. Just like you did when Emily came to see you and like Trapper had told me. The pastor's words when he read those Scripture verses had etched a place in my heart, and I couldn't forget them. I *am* going to spend eternity in heaven with you, Jackie. I know that now."

"Oh, Sam, you have no idea how happy that makes me. Of course I can forgive you."

Without warning, he stood and swung her up in his arms as his lips claimed hers in the sweetest kiss she'd ever experienced. She trembled against him, her tears wetting his shirt as she clung to him.

Jackie felt her heart racing. Sam. The love of her life. The only man she'd ever loved, and she was in his arms once again. "I wish you could've seen him, Sam," she murmured, her face pressed tightly against his strong chest.

Sam pulled her even closer. "Tell me about him. I–I need to know. I want to hear everything."

She drew in a deep breath. "Are you sure? Some of it's not very pretty."

He placed a gentle kiss on her forehead. "I'm sure."

Jackie breathed a quick prayer to God, asking Him for strength, then began her story. "I went for my regular visits to the doctor. Although most things seemed to be coming along okay, he was concerned because I was still spotting and carrying my placenta a bit low. But he told me it usually moved into place by itself. I guess you'd been gone about a month or so when I felt movement in my stomach. I knew right then it was our baby."

She looked up at him. "Oh, Sam, I can't begin to tell you what a feeling that was. By the time I went for my next checkup, he was moving all over the place. Because of my spotting and since my mother'd had high-risk pregnancies, the doctor decided to do an ultrasound. I didn't know what that was, but when I saw our baby moving around on that screen I shouted so loud I'm sure I scared the nurse out of her wits. Then the doctor asked if I wanted to know if it was a boy or a girl! Of course I answered *yes.* Well, it took a little bit of time; but finally Sammy moved into position, and we could tell he was a boy. I told the doctor I was going to name him Samuel Nathan Mulvaney, after you, Sam."

"I know." Sam gulped hard, his eyes blinking rapidly, tears rolling down his cheeks. "I read it in one of your notes."

In all the years she'd known him, she'd never seen him cry. He'd been too proud of his tough guy, macho man image to let his emotions get the better of him. She used to think it was from all the training he'd received in the army and from being around other military men with the same attitude.

"I can't begin to tell you how happy I was. I tried to phone the base in Germany, but you were on assignment. I wanted so much to share this wonderful experience with you. The doctor had even printed out Sammy's ultrasound picture so I could send it to you."

Sam nuzzled his chin in her hair. "Oh, Jackie. I'm so sorry."

She forced herself to continue. "I'd felt pretty good, but I suddenly began to feel tired. I'd put on quite a bit of weight, and I attributed it to that. Then I started spotting more heavily. When I called the doctor's office, they said spotting was fairly common and told me to come in the next morning." She paused. "I was scared, Sam, but aside from my so-called friends I had no one else to talk to."

"And I couldn't be reached."

She nodded. "Exactly. The spotting did slow down a bit, but then as I got out of bed at nearly dawn I began to hemorrhage. The sight of all that blood terrified me. All I could think about was getting help."

"And you drove yourself to the hospital instead of calling an ambulance or going to the doctor's office?"

"Yes, and since you've read my notes, you know what happened. I–I—"

He put a finger to her lips. "Shh, don't say it."

"I never dreamt the pain would be so severe. I thought I was dying, but I didn't care. All I could think about was that precious baby. I'd have gone through anything to keep him alive."

His warm breath struck her cheeks as he rested his forehead against hers.

"I–I didn't know—"

"They tried desperately to save him, Sam, but they—they couldn't."

Sam cupped her face between his hands and stroked her cheeks with his thumbs. "Oh, Jackie. Dear, sweet Jackie."

She drew a deep breath through numb lips. "Although he only weighed three pounds and two ounces, he was beautiful, Sam."

She smiled, the memory as fresh as if it were yesterday. "The doctor advised against my seeing him, but I had to do it. I had to! Finally, he agreed. I watched as the nurse cleaned up our baby and swaddled him. She even put a funny little hat on his head, like they do all newborns."

"Was he—did he—"

"He was perfectly formed. Ten teensy fingers and ten teensy toes, and his little face was like that of an angel." She let out a nervous giggle as she remembered how the little hat had nearly swallowed up his tiny head. "The nurse got her Polaroid camera and took pictures of him. Then she let me sit in the rocking chair and hold him, and she got pictures of the two of us."

Even through her tears, she could see Sam's lower lip quiver.

"Do—do you still have those pictures?"

"Yes, but I've packed them away in preparation for leaving Juneau."

"I'd like to see them."

Her heart pounded erratically at his words. "I was hoping, one day, you would. I even have the tiny little identification bracelet the hospital made for him, and I've framed his precious little foot and handprints."

Blinking, Sam rubbed the bridge of his nose with his thumb and forefinger. "I–I wish I'd been there with you. You shouldn't have had to go through that alone. We—were a family."

Jackie swallowed at the lump in her throat. "Our son would've been seventeen now, Sam, probably finishing up his junior year of high school."

Sam slipped his arm across her shoulders and rested his head against hers. "You think he would've been the star quarterback for his school's football team, as I was?"

She responded with a slight chuckle and reached a hand up to touch his cheek. "I'm sure of it. And he'd have driven all the girls crazy with his good looks."

She felt his chest rise and fall.

"I wish I could've seen him."

"He looked like he was sleeping, Sam. I kissed him and told him how much we had both wanted him to live, and I told him I'd named him Sammy, after you."

He drew in an audible breath and sent her a self-deprecating look. "I let you both down. Then, like a self-righteous fool, I came home from Germany and accused you of killing our baby. How you must've hated me."

"Your words only hurt me because I loved you so much."

Sam rose and began to pace about the room, his steps short and uneven, his hands flailing wildly through the air. "And I killed that love."

Suddenly, she was moving toward him, as if being drawn by a magnet. She flung her arms about his waist and hugged him tightly, resting her head against his strong back. "Don't you see, Sam? Nothing you could do could kill my love for you. Not even that! I loved you then. I love you now." Her words tumbled out before she could stop them.

Sam spun around in her arms and stared down at her. "You mean it? You still love me? After all—"

She touched a finger to his lips. "Yes. I'll always love you."

"Do—do you think there's even the slightest chance for us?"

She leaned into him, enjoying their closeness as she pressed her face to his shoulder. "Do you?"

He slid a finger beneath her chin, lifting her face to his, his still-youthful eyes blazing with a passion she'd thought had long ago been lost. "I'd give anything to have you back as my wife."

Jackie's eyes filled with fresh tears as she gave him a coy smile. "Anything?" She watched as his lips moved slowly toward hers and he hovered tantalizingly close. She felt the same old flutter of excitement she'd felt on their wedding day when they'd enjoyed their first kiss as husband and wife.

"Anything," he whispered against her lips. "Jackie, will you marry me all over again? Be my wife?"

twelve

"Ma–marry you?"

She stared at him with startled exhilaration. Never had she expected to hear those words again from Sam.

"Will you, Jackie? I know I have no right to ask, not after the way I've behaved, but you said you'd forgive me and—"

She couldn't contain her smile. It was her decision now. He'd been the one to end their marriage the first time. Now, all these years later, it was up to her to decide if that marriage could be rekindled. But one thing still bothered her. She looked longingly into his face. "Oh, Sam, I want desperately to say yes, but I–I don't know. The doctor never said for sure—but I may not be able to give you children. I don't even know if I'd ever be able to carry a baby to full term—" She slowly lifted her eyes to meet his. "And I'm over forty now."

A hint of a grin tilted the corners of his mouth. "Hey, Kiddo, we're both over forty now. As much as I'd like to have had children, that's the last thing I'm concerned about now." He gave a boyish shrug. "But if it happens, it happens!"

Slowly she placed her hand in his and smiled up at him as old feelings of love surrounded her heart. "Then, yes, Sam, my answer is yes!"

He wrapped his arms about her so tightly she found it difficult to draw in a breath as she gazed into his eyes.

"I don't have much to offer you, Jackie. As soon as I see Trapper, I'll be out of a job. I don't own any property. I don't even have a rented apartment back in Memphis to offer you. I'm sure many men could lay much more at your feet, if you'd let them. But I promise to love, honor, and cherish you for the rest of our lives."

Jackie's vision became fuzzy as she looked into his handsome face, the face that had haunted her dreams for the past seventeen years. Could this, too, be a dream? Would she wake up in her bed, only to find she was alone in her dark, empty room? She wanted to freeze this moment in time, to remember it forever.

"Being with you, spending the rest of our years together—that's all I ask. You're the only man I've ever loved or wanted as my husband. I'm sure God designed us to be together. Only He could have performed a miracle and brought us both to Juneau like this."

His misty gaze never left her face. "I don't deserve you, Sweetheart, but with God's help I know we can make it. I want to be the kind of man God wants me to be. A man like Trapper. I want to be the husband you deserve."

His words flowed over her like a crystal river, blanketing her, engulfing her, bathing her with the love she desired. She watched as a slow smile crept across his face, and despite any misgivings she might have had, she knew she could trust this man with her very life.

He pulled her forward and cradled her to him as his warm lips planted tiny kisses at her temple, her eyelids, then the tip of her nose. She clung to him as if he were her lifeline, her hands splaying across his back, her fingers fanning out across his broad, muscled shoulders.

"I love you, Jackie Mulvaney," he whispered, his words feathering her ear.

His close proximity played havoc with her senses. She could feel her heart beating in time with his, and it was a delicious feeling. Her whole body shivered as he lowered his mouth onto hers, and she melted into his arms, absorbing his masculine scent. Gone were all the thoughts of getting her things packed in time to catch her afternoon flight out of Juneau. Gone were the feelings of hurt and disappointment she'd felt for over seventeen years. Nothing else occupied her thoughts but her love for this man, the joy of being in his arms once again and the anticipation of becoming his wife, as she returned his kisses.

Finally, Sam pulled away slightly, his arms still circling her waist as he gazed into her eyes. "We'd better hurry if we're going to fly out of here today."

She gave him a startled look. "Y–you're going with me? Now?"

"Yes, it's the only way." He motioned toward the empty boxes she'd brought back from the supermarket. "Go ahead with your packing. I'm going to tell Trapper we're leaving."

"He already knows, Sam. I should've told you earlier. I invited Trapper and Glorianna, his parents, and the Gordons over last night. They know the whole story."

Sam rubbed at his forehead and let out a heavy sigh. "I'm sure they think I'm nothing but a scoundrel now that they know about Sammy and that I was your husband."

"My intent wasn't to make you look bad, Sam. I explained it was my fault for being so insistent about having an abortion."

A slow smile of understanding crept across his face. "I know that, Sweetie. I'd expect that from you. They deserved to know the truth. I'm leaving Trapper in a bind, but now that he knows why, I'm sure he'll understand. I do want to let him know I've gotten my life straightened out with God. That man has been praying for me."

"He's a fine man. He'll be glad to hear it."

Sam gave her a quick peck on the cheek. "Facing him is going to be hard, but I can't put it off. I'm going to see him now; then I'll head over to Grandma's Feather Bed, throw my things in my suitcase, and call the airport for reservations. I'll be back as quick as I can."

He kissed her once more, then pulled on his jacket and headed for the door, reminding her again, "I love you!"

❧

Jackie hurried to the window and watched as Sam slid into the rental car, started the engine, and headed off toward the Timberwolf house. Everything had happened so fast, so unexpectedly. She'd crawled out of bed that very morning, brokenhearted, despondent, and feeling as if her life were coming to an end. But, thanks to God, that was not to be. Sam was back in her life for good, and she would soon become his wife.

After putting a CD in the player, she flitted around the house, humming to the music as she placed things in each box, sealing it with packing tape, and labeling its contents. When she was finished, she danced into the kitchen, whirling and pirouetting and singing along with the lead singer on the CD, her joy bubbling over uncontrollably. She'd just poured herself a glass of juice when she heard a knock on the door.

Sam's back!

Jackie opened the door and gasped. It was Sam all right,

but he had an entire entourage with him.

He gave her a lopsided grin as he gestured toward the little group, and they all moved inside. "I tried to talk them out of it, but they insisted on coming."

"It was Trapper's idea," Glorianna said proudly, holding onto her husband's arm.

"Yeah," Hank chimed in, reaching for Tina's hand. "He said friends needed to rally around each other in a time of need, and we *are* your friends, Jackie, both yours *and* Sam's."

Tina giggled as she rubbed her slightly rounded tummy. "This little guy is gonna need an uncle Sam and an auntie Jackie."

Jackie frowned. What were they saying?

Emily moved quickly to her side and wrapped an arm about her shoulders. "You didn't think you were gonna get away from us that easily, did you?" She motioned to her husband, who was standing silently by the door. "Come on over here, Dyami. Tell this girl how much she means to us."

The elder man shuffled across the floor and took Jackie's hand in his, patting it in a fatherly way. "We love you, Girl. God loves you, too. Don't ever forget it."

Jackie smiled at each one through her tears. "I love all of you, but—why are you here?"

Sam pulled her from Emily and into his arms. "They want us to stay, Sweetheart, both of us. Glorianna wants you to stay on as the manager of her shop, and Trapper still wants me as his business partner. Can you believe it?"

Six people encircled them, their arms entwined with one another's.

"It's unanimous," Trapper said, speaking for all six. "We want you both to stay. I've got big plans, and they include

Sam and that helicopter we want to buy."

Sam grinned. "Yeah. Mulvaney-Timberwolf Aviation."

"How about Timberwolf-Mulvaney Aviation?" Trapper shot back, an exaggerated smile peeking through his heavy mustache and beard.

Sam uttered a playful snort. "I can live with that."

Trapper's face took on a seriousness Jackie had rarely seen on him. "What you did, Jackie—lying to us all these years—was wrong. But, considering the circumstances, I think all of us understand and have accepted it. You were covering up a painful part of your life. A part you wanted to put behind you. We couldn't fault you for that. Most of us have things in our lives we'd prefer to forget."

Glorianna gave her a sweet smile. "You could've told me, Jackie, once we became friends. I'd have been disappointed, but I wouldn't have thought any less of you. I could tell that first day I met you there was something troubling about you, a leave-me-alone type of attitude that bothered me. I knew you resented me because of Trapper, but it was more than that. I didn't know what, but that's hindsight, isn't it? Please know we all love you, Honey and want both you and Sam to stay. The Bear Paw's customers would never forgive me if I let you get away."

Trapper's smile returned. "Besides, you have God to turn to now. Sam tells me he's accepted the Lord, too. Nothing could please us more. Glorianna and I have been praying for both of you." He nodded toward his parents. "Mom and Dad have, too."

"So have Tina and I," Hank added. "You two are very special to us."

"Buck and Victoria Silverbow have had you on their prayer

list, too," Trapper interjected. "I can't wait to tell them the two of you have not only accepted the Lord, but you're back together. Only God could have worked that one out."

Jackie found herself speechless. Yesterday she'd felt rejected and alone. Now Sam was back in her life, and so were her friends. God was truly good.

Sam gave her a loving squeeze as his smile broadened. "What's the answer, Sweetheart? It's up to you. Glorianna says we can stay right here in this apartment, if you like. Or we can get our own house. I'll be happy living anywhere, as long as I'm sharing that home with you."

"Stay," Tina said, reaching a hand across the circle. "Please. It wouldn't be the same without you."

"Yeah, stay. I need those big bucks you and Trapper are going to pay me for being the Mulvaney-Timberwolf"—Hank paused and gave them a big grin—"or the Timberwolf-Mulvaney attorney. Whichever name you decide on."

Still finding it hard to speak, her heart running over with love for these wonderful friends, Jackie looked from one kind face to the next, then back to Sam. "Let's stay!"

❧

"Up a couple of inches," Jackie told Sam a month later as he held the little quilt against their bedroom wall. "Now over just a bit."

"Here?" he asked, after making the slight adjustment. "Make sure this is where you want it before I drill the holes in the wall."

She backed up a couple of steps and squinted her eyes. "It's perfect."

Sam took a pencil from his pocket and made two small marks on the wall, then lowered the quilt. "Honey, are you sure seeing this quilt on the wall every day won't make you sad? It holds a lot of memories."

She carefully took the little blue and white quilt from his hands and held it out to admire. "How could it make me sad? I made it as a memorial to our son. To Sammy."

Sam stepped up behind her and wrapped his arms about her, nestling his chin in her hair. "I'm glad you made it, but I'm really happy you wrote those sweet notes to him. If I hadn't come to your apartment that morning and found your door unlocked and barged my way in, I might never have seen those quilt blocks or the notes, and I would've lost you. You could've flown out of Juneau, and I'd never have found you again."

"It was God's doing, Sam. I'm sure of it. The last thing I wanted was for you to find those quilt blocks. I'd been so careful to keep them hidden under my bed all the time I was working on them. They were between Sammy and me, and no one else. Especially not you."

"I hadn't planned to come to your apartment that morning. I didn't even know you'd already told everyone about our lies. But I woke up early and couldn't go back to sleep. All I could think about were the awful things I'd said to you before I left for Skagway. I didn't want you to leave without at least telling you I was sorry."

He spun her around in his arms and captured her face between his palms, his blue eyes reaching into the very center of her heart. "And when I knocked and you didn't answer, I nearly turned away and started down the stairs, but something deep within me told me to check the door. I did and found it standing open just a crack. I hadn't even noticed it when I'd knocked. I knew you'd be upset if I went in while you were gone, but I had to see you. We'd already parted bitterly once. I couldn't let that happen again."

"Oh, Sam, what if you'd gone on that morning, before I got back home?" Just the thought struck panic to her heart.

"But I didn't, Sweetheart. I know now it was God speaking to me, making me stay. He wants us together, Jackie. I think He created us for each other."

"I think so, too." Jackie stood on tiptoe and planted a kiss on her husband's lips.

His hand caressed her cheek. "You were the most beautiful bride I've ever seen. Even more beautiful than you were the first time I married you!"

She was sure she was blushing. "I was amazed at how many of our new Christian friends were at our wedding. I think the whole church was there."

He nodded. "I'm glad the Silverbows were able to make it. They're nice folks. I'm sure we'll get better acquainted with them when I begin to do those wonderful missionary flights into the bush with Trapper and Hank."

Jackie gave him a teasing smile. "You'd do those things for free?"

A hint of amusement quirked at his lips. "For free for God!"

"I made this little quilt for our son, Sam," she said dreamily as she pulled away and let her fingers trace the intricate stitching on one of the quilt's blocks. "I only wish I could have wrapped it about him."

Sam pulled her into his arms again and cradled her head against his chest. "I know, Sweetheart. I do, too."

She tilted her head up a little, regarding him thoughtfully as she clung to the little quilt. "I never want us to forget about

Sammy. This little quilt will always serve as a reminder of him. He was a part of us, Sam, and we were a part of him. As you said, my dear husband, this baby quilt is a symbol of our love."

Sam kissed her cheek, then pulled away and pointed toward the wall where he'd made the pencil marks. "Sure that's where you want me to hang it?"

She nodded as she gazed at her husband. "Absolutely sure."

She watched lovingly as he headed toward the shed to get the drill. She and Sam were together again.

This time for keeps.

A Letter To Our Readers

Dear Reader:

In order that we might better contribute to your reading enjoyment, we would appreciate your taking a few minutes to respond to the following questions. We welcome your comments and read each form and letter we receive. When completed, please return to the following:

Fiction Editor
Heartsong Presents
PO Box 719
Uhrichsville, Ohio 44683

1. Did you enjoy reading *The Baby Quilt* by Joyce Livingston?
   ❑ Very much! I would like to see more books by this author!
   ❑ Moderately. I would have enjoyed it more if
   ____
   ____
   ____

2. Are you a member of **Heartsong Presents**? ❑ Yes ❑ No
   If no, where did you purchase this book? ______________
   ____

3. How would you rate, on a scale from 1 (poor) to 5 (superior), the cover design? ______________

4. On a scale from 1 (poor) to 10 (superior), please rate the following elements.

   ____ Heroine ____ Plot
   ____ Hero ____ Inspirational theme
   ____ Setting ____ Secondary characters

5. These characters were special because?__________________

____

____

6. How has this book inspired your life?__________________

____

____

7. What settings would you like to see covered in future **Heartsong Presents** books? __________________

____

____

8. What are some inspirational themes you would like to see treated in future books? __________________

____

____

9. Would you be interested in reading other **Heartsong Presents** titles? ❑ Yes ❑ No

10. Please check your age range:

❑ Under 18	❑ 18-24
❑ 25-34	❑ 35-45
❑ 46-55	❑ Over 55

Name______________________________________

Occupation __________________________________

Address ____________________________________

City________________ State______ Zip__________